Mosi-oa-Tunya

THE
THUNDERING
SMOKE

BOOK THREE
THE END OF THE LINE

GUY QUIGLEY

The Thundering Smoke
Book Three: The End of the Line
Copyright 2025 by Guy Quigley

ISBN 978-1-967421-22-0 (Paperback)
ISBN 978-1-967421-23-7 (Hardback)
ISBN 978-1-967421-21-3 (eBook)

Printed in the United States of America

This is a work of fiction. Names, characters, places, and incidents either are the product of the author's imagination or are used fictitiously. Any resemblance to actual events or locales or persons, living or dead, is entirely coincidental.

Published by ThunderSmoke Media LLC

DEDICATIONS

This book is dedicated to my wonderful wife Wendy, a true child of Africa, my soul mate, partner, mother of my children, and best friend for over fifty-four years.

ACKNOWLEDGEMENTS

To my parents, Joseph Quigley and Mother Josephine Quigley, the ulti-mate thespians. He was a violin virtuoso who was as comfortable playing the classics as he was an Irish jig. While she was an exceptional actress/ director who could watch a film and later write the script from memory. These guiding lights taught me the art of self-expression. Without their love, knowledge, encouragement, and early guidance, this novel may never have been possible (RIP)

AND

To my mother-in-law, Stella Horton, a sophisticated lady and healer with significant hands-on knowledge about Africa and its wildlife. Also, thanks to my father-in-law George Horton, the finest hunter I have ever known with bush skills that were unquestionable. I savor those many nights spent around a roaring campfire while lions mated in the distance, hearing countless true stories stranger than fiction. And to the many col-lectively unknown who helped shape this story. (RIP)

AND

A very special thank you to my eldest daughter Claudine Quigley Piechotta, who embarked on the amazing and time-consuming challenge of editing and adapting this manuscript. With her input and prowess, she painlessly and graciously undertook the task of rewriting my manuscript. A very special and talented lady.

ABOUT THE AUTHOR

Guy Quigley was born in Ireland to a second-generation thespian family. He was educated in Ireland, where he left the theatre and entered the business world. He is married with three children and has six grandchildren. From 1970 through the early 80s, he built a 40,000-acre cattle ranch in Zambia, Africa housing 5,000 heads of cattle and imported 100 pedigree Semmintaler cattle from Bavaria, Germany, via three Boeing 707 Skybarn aircraft, establishing the first pedigree Semmintaler stud in the south-central African country.

In his spare time, he wrote two fictional novels — one, a children's story, *The Little People*, and the other, a historical fiction saga, *The Smoke That Thunders*; now after over forty years is being published as a trilogy.

In the United States, he successfully developed and marketed an award-winning cold remedy zinc lozenge under the franchise name COLD-EEZE,® establishing the US zinc-lozenge marketplace. To market the product, he formed The Quigley Corporation in 1989 which became a public entity on February 7, 1991, trading on the NASDAQ under the symbol (QGLY). His product COLD-EEZE® is available throughout the United States. He retired in 2009 and returned to his writing which has been of tremendous therapeutic value and comes full circle to his birth roots. He has written three more books, *The Rebel Son with an* (Audio Book), *Hellevator* and a soon to be published cold-war spy thriller *Predators at the Gates,* which will also be available as an audio book. Along with his novels he has written several award-winning movie scripts. In his film production endeavors, He is the ex- producer of *Magic Boys* (*Diamond Heist*) in the EU. He is also the ex- producer of the spoof *Breaking Wind* and the ex-producer of *Wicked Blood.* Utilizing his ThunderSmoke Media Company he produced the 2015 award-winning movie *Apparition.* His latest film production from ThunderSmoke Media is *Impuratus,* a thriller horror movie, due for release in North America and world-wide distribution October 2023.

www.guyquigley.com www.thundersmokefilms.com

PREFACE

For over a decade, along with my wife, I owned and operated a cattle ranch in the south-central African country of Zambia. Without TV and little reliable world news, we were somewhat cloistered and spent most evenings listening to true stories dating back to the last century. Coming from an Irish thespian background did not make me the ideal worker of the land, yet I learned the hard way by trial and error.

My motivation to write a book stemmed from the endless stories I learned. Hence, at every spare moment I had, I started to handwrite my story utilizing my knowledge of Ireland, her history, and the Africa I came to know, love, and attempt to weave them together in an action-adventure love story. After a couple of chapters, it all seemed to fall into place, and I could not wait to put more words on paper, albeit they were barely legible from my terrible art of scribbling.

So was born my story of a fictional character called Tom Sutton, who during the Irish liberation war of 1919, under the inspiration of Michael Collins – the top Irish revolutionary leader of the time – was overtly successful in his execution of disrupting British rule. Being a man with price on his head, he loses his wife Grace - the love of his life - in a brutal rape executed by Black and Tans at a bloody raid on his home.

Believing his son Sean suffered the same deadly fate as Grace he is forced to escape and by sheer misunderstanding, he finds himself on the vast continent of Africa, sinking into the shame and degradation of alcohol. By a strange twist of fate, a little girl with a bowl of soup and the fear of the loss of her dying father brings him back from living death to the reality of the child's pain and future.

Together with the young girl Heidi and Weasel Byrne, his only friend from the Irish troubled times, they travel north through the small working goldmines of Southern Rhodesia to the north of Mosi-oa-Tunya (The Smoke That Thunders-Victoria falls), finally settling in Northern Rhodesia. There, a new life of intrigue, crime, adventure, and love is born until his past comes back to haunt him.

My problem in writing a novel was the fact that it was handwritten, and two-finger typed. There were no computers back in the mid-seventies, so errors abounded. It took over eighteen months to get my writing into some form of the legible manuscript. So, what did I learn from such experience? Patience is definitely a virtue.

The story in my mind was chapters ahead of what was being handwritten. Several times, there was a writer's block. That taught me to think hard and continue to write, even if nobody liked it. This book was my first attempt at writing, and since then, I have written three other books and several screenplays.

CONTENTS

CHAPTER 1

THE END OF THE LINE

Tom's palms sweated in anticipation of Heidi's arrival. It had been a whole year since he had seen her, and so much had changed in his own life. He couldn't wait to share the good news with her about Demberra and the King property. The train couldn't arrive at Bulawayo fast enough. Maria had stayed at home preparing a dinner of monumental proportion for Heidi's homecoming. She was really trying, and that made him happy. He believed that she genuinely wanted Heidi to like her, to be her friend. He desperately wanted that too, and there was no reason in his mind that they shouldn't hit it off splendidly.

When Heidi stepped off the train, she beamed a rosy, red lip-stick smile at him, dropped her bags, and instantly threw herself into his arms. It was just like the old days. If it didn't cause a scene, he would have spun her around like he did when she was little. She had grown up a lot in a year. Her hair was now cut in the style of the day, coiffed in blond curls that framed her cherub face. Her blue eyes were as bright as ever, and her cheeks were rosy with a touch of blush. Her clothes were modern but sensible, a navy blue fitted skirt ensemble, a white blouse, and low black heels. She was comfortable in her skin, he thought. Her independent streak as a child had caught up with her, and she had become a formidable young woman.

"My darling, Heidi! It is so good to see you. Dear Lord, I missed you so much, my girl. I have so much to tell you!" Tom exuberated as he gathered up her bags.

They stopped overnight at the hotel as they had done before, but it didn't take long for Heidi to scold him for dinner that evening.

"You know there was no need for you to come all the way to Bulawayo, Uncle Tom. I know my way back to Demberra well enough."

"Well, I had a few errands to run in Livingstone, so it wasn't a bother to catch the train here."

"It's a half-a-day trip at least." she laughed, dabbing the corners of her mouth with the napkin.

"Besides, Maria wanted me out of the house, so she could prepare for your arrival." Tom figured it was a good idea to start ingratiating her to Maria before they arrived home.

Heidi quickly changed the subject and launched into a story about her first teaching assignment and her final exam, chattering on without giving him a chance to interject." Tom decided it was best to just let her talk. There would be plenty of time on the long ride home to Demberra tomorrow to have a deeper conversation, besides, they were both tired.

Since they were anxious to get back to the farm, they decided to stay on the train straight through to Demberra. It was Bert and Charlie's day off, so the train ride was quite uneventful. Once her luggage was stowed and they were settled in their seats, Heidi removed her hat and gloves and kicked off her left shoe.

Old habits die hard, thought Tom as he chuckled at her bare foot.

"You still hate wearing shoes, eh? Even those fancy heels?"

"That's right!" said Heidi as she flicked off the other into his lap and laughed wildly, causing the couple behind them to clear their throats and mumble in disapproval.

"Must you cause a ruckus every time you ride this train, young woman?" said Tom in a mocking reprimand.

"Someone has to keep you on your toes, Uncle."

"That is true." agreed Tom

So, tell me about her, Uncle Tom. What is she like?

"Who? Maria?" asked Tom, caught off guard.

"Yes, your wife."

"She is not my wife, Heidi."

"But I thought?"

"I don't remember writing any such thing to you, Heidi."

"Does this mean you are living in sin, Uncle Tom?" gasped Heidi, aloud exaggerating the word SIN dramatically, as the couple ahead of them again whispered in disgust. Heidi was enjoying watching her uncle squirm a little, and humor was the only way she'd get herself through this, she thought.

"I don't understand how whenever I travel with you, we always manage to have an audience from start to finish."

"Phew, I'm just relieved to know that you aren't married to her because you belong to me forever," Heidi said with dramatic seriousness and a wide grin as she leaned in to face him. He shifted nervously in his seat.

"This whole conversation is very heavy. I think I'll have a cigarette," she said affirmatively as she pulled a small decorative case from her bag, snapped it open, and retrieved a stick. She placed it between her shiny lips and lit the end, inhaling and exhaling a stream of smoke. Tom's mouth hung noticeably open.

"Want one?" she asked nonchalantly. He declined. "When did you start to smoke, little girl?"

"Only to keep up with you and your cigars." she mocked as she exhaled another puff of smoke into the air between them. This was a battle he would not win, he decided. At least not today.

"Maria…she is in love with me, Heidi," he said, trying to steer the conversation back to a serious tone.

"Hmm, but do you love her, Uncle Tom?" asked Heidi with sincerity and a raised eyebrow.

"She is a wonderful woman, you'll see," said Tom with finality, strategically avoiding the question.

"Oh, and the biggest news, what I wanted to tell you last night. Demberra is ours and the King Place, too." exclaimed Tom, clearly wishing to avoid any further conversation about his actual feelings.

Heidi took the cue. She knew that Tom had wanted to discuss Maria with her last night, but she just wasn't ready for it. And even though she couldn't help feeling jealous, she knew intimately of Tom's past and was happy that he had found someone to share his life with. She admittedly wasn't thrilled that Demberra would never be as it once was, and this new woman would now share his time. It had, after all, always been just the two of them against the world. She had been the yin to his yang, the pepper to his salt, and now all that would change.

But Heidi intuitively had always known that this day would eventually come, even when she was little. And she had had Tom's undivided attention for longer than she expected. But now that it was here, she was feeling the loss in inextricable ways. But she had promised herself that she would try and like this woman, for his sake if nothing else. After all, she couldn't be that bad if she had fallen in love with her Uncle Tom. She must have seen the same vulnerability in him that Heidi had been so keenly aware of all those years ago. For that alone, she might be redeemable, thought Heidi. She smiled and reached for his hand.

"How wonderful, tell me all about it." Heidi entreated.

They spent the remainder of the trip discussing all that had occurred at Demberra since Tom's last letter. Heidi almost laughed herself off the seat as he retold the part about Simalala, the drunk herder and the blue-eyed man. Tom purposefully left out some of the violence in his altercation with Bradley.

"Suffice it to say, he knows not to mess with me...with us anymore," he said in conclusion right as the train pulled into Kabi Siding. Maria was waiting for them and waved at them from the top of the hill. Tom swallowed the lump in his throat.

As they made their way up the hill to the house, in the scotch cart with all of Heidi's bags, Maria remained on the verandah waving and smiling, giving it her all. Heidi turned to Tom with one eyebrow raised, as she always did in jest.

"Come on now," said Tom. "Give her a chance. She deserves at least that. She's been through a lot, and she wants to get along. Wait until you see her vegetable garden."

"You mean MY vegetable garden." insisted Heidi with a tinge of resentment.

"Yes, of course, lass…your garden. In fact, she does call it YOUR garden. She's taken really good care of it. And Soleil too… she's a horsewoman, you know and has cared for your pony as you would have yourself," said Tom honestly.

"Alright, I will be good, Uncle Tom…for your sake." Heidi acquiesced with a smile and squeezed his hand.

When Heidi dismounted the cart, Maria was there to greet her. She was more striking than her uncle had let on. With her deep brown eyes, flawless olive skin, long raven hair, and trim figure, she understood in an instant why her Uncle Tom was smitten. Maria threw her arms around Heidi without hesitation and embraced her like a long-lost sister.

"Welcome back home Heidi. I have been waiting for so long to meet you." Maria said warmly.

"Likewise," said Heidi more formally. "You have made yourself at home here, no doubt, over the past year and a half?" suggested Heidi with a sarcastic edge. Tom threw her a look as he gathered her things and gave Maria a peck on the cheek as he passed.

Maria either missed the sarcasm completely or simply chose to rise above it, the latter of which annoyed Heidi more.

"Your Uncle Tom and I have been very happy here, thank you. I have tried to take care of Demberra in your absence the way I suspect you would. I feel so fortunate to be able to wake up each morning in this beautiful place." smiled Maria.

"Thank you," said Heidi with reluctant sincerity. This woman genuinely tried to befriend her. And she had no real reason to reject her. She had to try and let her bitterness go, she thought. She couldn't expect Tom to remain single his entire life. If this was the woman he had chosen, she had better attempt to like her, or she feared she would lose Tom in the process.

After a tour of the house, complete with Christmas decorations in every room and a trip out to the vegetable garden and stable, Heidi had to admit that Maria had taken exceptional care of Demberra and that she must deeply love Tom, who hadn't yet made their union official. She, for one would not want to live that way, and she felt oddly sorry for Maria and disappointed in her uncle.

"You know she is far more beautiful than you described, Thomas," said Maria as they waited for Heidi's arrival at dinner that night. Heidi didn't disappoint. She arrived at dinner in a cornflower blue silk dress, her hair perfectly styled and just enough makeup to accentuate her eyes and punctuate her pouty lips. She even wore shoes, which was a first. Maria was excited to unveil her three-course Portuguese meal, and it did not go unappreciated. She was an excellent cook, and Heidi couldn't deny that Jonas had come a long way since their cooking "experiments" two years ago.

Tom was a mere observer at this tennis match between the ladies, beaming ear to ear as they bantered on about cooking, gardening, and horses. By the end of the evening, the conversation had become easy and even peppered with laughter. As Tom had suspected and hoped, these two women were beginning to realize how much alike they were, and Heidi had come to understand why Tom had chosen Maria. She was independent yet affectionate. She was funny and even a little hot-headed, which Tom needed. And she obviously loved Demberra and Tom with her whole being, and Heidi couldn't fault her there.

"I am happy for you, Maria. My Uncle Tom is a good man," whispered Heidi as they all departed for bed that night. Maria smiled and squeezed her hand. The ice had been officially broken.

They enjoyed a festive Christmas together, thanks to all of Maria's efforts. Heidi had to admit that aside from her early childhood Christmases with her father and mother, which had nearly faded from memory, and her special Christmas in Capetown with Tom and Weasel, this one was the best!

Maria wasn't smothering and took care to give Tom and Heidi their space. She seemed just as happy in the garden or kitchen as she was in their company, and Heidi appreciated that. They had taken to riding together most days. Sometimes they would take a picnic along and be out all day, sharing each other's histories and dreams for the future under the shade of a favourite tree. After a few weeks, both women had come to realize that they each had somehow filled a void in the other's life.

One Sunday morning in early February, Tom was set to take the train to Livingstone for a day trip. Weasel was in town, and they had planned to meet. Bert and Charlie had joined them for a hearty breakfast that morning, which had been the custom in years past, albeit less frequently these days. With a more robust train schedule, the pair found little time for leisurely visits. Now that Heidi had traversed adolescence, these occasional visits with Bert and Charlie were also no longer awkward for her, and Maria's presence only aided in creating equilibrium and deflating any rumours of impropriety between Tom and his ward.

When the train pulled out that morning with Tom en route to Livingstone, Maria and Heidi sat on the verandah drinking coffee and waving at the men as they disappeared out of view.

"Do you know anything about the three men who robbed Simalala's father's cattle two summers ago?" Maria asked curiously, out of nowhere.

"I only know of Bradley. Obviously, you are aware that he tried to swindle my Uncle Tom out of Demberra. Why do you ask?" replied Heidi fervently.

"Yes, I know about Bradley, of course, and the history, but I'm not sure I told you the whole story about that day," Maria said in a whisper, wishing to unburden her secret.

"What do you mean Maria?" asked Heidi intrigued.

"As you know, this whole thing happened right before I came to Demberra for the first time. The men have so bloodied Heidi after we cut them down. I was so scared. I didn't think they would survive. I had to pretend to be strong. I didn't want your uncle to think I was weak. After all, we barely knew each other then. So, I muscled all the courage I could come up with. It took a lot of time to tend to their wounds and get them in shape enough to travel."

"That's awful. I didn't know all the details. Some of the African customs can be quite brutal. I can't imagine what it must have been like. But those men were thieves, after all, they sort of deserved it don't you think? You and Uncle Tom and Similala were like the Samaritans, really." Maria nodded in agreement.

"I mean, you could have just walked away after what they did. Did you ever find out who those men were, Maria? I mean, were they just Bradley's henchmen? Uncle Tom wouldn't tell me any more than that. I suppose he didn't want me to worry."

"Yes, they all worked for Bradley, that's true. "Bloody," Bradley as Tom calls him. But that's what I wanted to tell you, Heidi. One of them, the youngest one…well, there was something different about him. He isn't a common criminality, and I have to say I felt really sorry for him that day."

"Go on," insisted Heidi intrigued.

"His name is John Siddley. A handsome young British man. He travelled to Livingstone from Salisbury, where his father was a government official. He came here searching for an adventure."

"Well, he certainly found it, didn't he? Must be a rogue then if he was working for Bradley! Or at the least a poor judge of character." Heidi scoffed, passing final judgment on the man.

"I don't know about that. He said he thought it would be an adventure. I just think he just got caught up with the wrong men."

"You seem to know a lot about this, John Siddley. What makes you think he isn't a common criminal like the rest or just a fool?" said Heidi suspiciously.

Maria took a couple of sips of her coffee and paused.

"Well, that is because I remained in touch with him, Heidi. After the incident, his father brought him back to Salisbury to recoup. We wrote to each other off and on, and frankly, I was shocked when he arrived back in Livingstone a couple of months ago. Before you came home for Christmas, Tom and I made several trips to Livingstone for supplies and things. When Tom was off conducting business for the farm, I met John for coffee a few times. I still don't understand why he came back here after what happened. But he has a job at the bank now, and I think he's trying to make his own way. Maybe he just likes Livingstone."

"That does seem strange after what happened," interjected Heidi.

"He is still ashamed of how we first met and doesn't like to talk about it. But I will say he's a good conversationalist about most things: culture, politics, music, you name it. He's also travelled quite a lot for one so young. He's your age. Well, maybe a year or two older. He's even quite funny, but he's lost somehow. I haven't told anyone about this but you. I had to get it off my chest. Tom would not be happy that I have stayed in contact with him. But I think Tom's wrong about him. Will you keep my secret?"

"Hmm," said Heidi pursing her lips. "So, you said this young man lives in Livingstone? Maria nodded.

"Because I would like to meet this gentleman friend of yours!"

"So, you'll keep my secret?"

"If I can meet him," said Heidi suggestively

"I could bring you along. But you'll see that there are wounds that run deep. Even though he can talk about a lot of things, he's a bit of a closed book, if you know what I mean. He lost his mother at a young age, so I suspect he had a difficult childhood- maybe that's it. He won't talk about it."

"That is something all three of us have in common then," stated Heidi earnestly, revisiting many a picnic conversation she and Maria had shared about growing up as girls without mothers.

"Do you know it was me who initially wrote to his father after the incident and told him to come and retrieve his son?" Maria said in a whisper as if the walls might hear.

"You wrote to his father? You are sneakier than I thought. Did he find out it twas you?" Heidi exclaimed, clasping her hands in delight, enjoying the intrigue more with each divulsion.

"I did eventually tell him. He was angry with me at first, but he's since forgiven me. It was for his own good, after all. I didn't want him to be around Bradley and his crew, and he needed to be cared for."

"Sweet Lord, Maria!" exclaimed Heidi, her eyes bright with engagement. "Do you still communicate with his father?"

"Yes, I have written to him a couple of times since he returned to Livingstone. He asked me to keep an eye on John. I'm sure he thinks I'm just a doting female who probably has romantic feelings for his son. Maybe I should be signing the letters "Thomas Edward Sutton," and then he might take me seriously." she laughed

"Now that would be a gas!" laughed Heidi, imagining how angry Tom would be if he found out. She liked the fact that Maria had included her in this secret.

"You have my confidence, Maria. Now when can I meet this sullen young adventurer," said Heidi patting Maria's hand across the table.

"Soon," promised Maria.

The women sat talking and smoking all night, waiting for the train. It rumbled past Kabi Siding at midnight, never slowed, and no one disembarked.

"Don't worry about Uncle Tom. He probably just got tied up in Livingstone and decided to spend the night," suggested Heidi, trying not to sound worried as they watched the train disappear into the inky night.

"He said he would be back today, though," Maria said, creasing her eyebrows. "He always rings me on the telephone if he is going to stay on."

"Well, all we can do now is go to bed and wait until morning. It's too late to ring the hotel now, and the desk will be closed." Heidi said encouragingly.

Both women parted ways reluctantly and retired to their bedrooms, eager for morning to come. At six-thirty, the phone jingled and then rang incessantly until both Maria and Heidi stood over it in anticipation. Maria lifted the receiver.

"Maria? Hello?"

"Good morning?"

"This is Leonard, Maria."

"Yes, Leonard, is everything alright? Heidi and I are worried. Have you seen Tom?"

"It's Leonard," mouthed Maria to Heidi.

"Maria! Maria! Are you there? Hello, can you hear me?"

"Yes, yes, Leonard, I can hear you."

"I am so sorry these phone lines are never good. The boys, Tom and Weasel, got quite rowdy last night, if you know what I mean. They were drinking as early as seven, and by nine, they were three sheets to the wind. Bonkers…if you catch my drift. There was some altercation at the bar that ended in a Scotsman with a black eye.

Then I caught wind from some witnesses that they were parading around near the Falls, with talk of trying to walk the handrail of the bridge. I threatened them with a night in jail, and they settled for a room at The Northwestern. So, they are at the hotel sleeping it off. I just didn't want you to worry."

"Thank you, Leonard. That was kind of you…we were worried."

"They will likely be on the next train home, Maria." clarified Len.

"No, please tell them to stay put. Heidi and I will come to Livingstone and bring them home. We have some business to attend to in town anyway." Maria winked at Heidi.

"So, who are the damsels in distress now, eh?" said Len with a chuckle. "I'll be sure to deliver the message, and you two ladies drive safely."

"We will, of course, and thank you!" said Maria, and she hung up the phone. Heidi shrugged her shoulders, looking for details.

"Pack a bag, Heidi, we are off to Livingstone to rescue Tom and Weasel and maybe pay a certain young man a visit. I'll fill you in on the way."

Later that morning at the Northwestern, Weasel and Tom emerged from their room and fumbled their way to the verandah, both nursing splitting headaches.

"Morning, boys! Glad to see you are up and about. You should be glad I didn't lock the two of you up last night for disorderly conduct. But lucky for you, I have a full house at the station. I have brought you both the remedy that you seek; gourmet police station black coffee."

Tom turned up his nose, but Weasel graciously accepted the flask of coffee. Before Weasel could take a swig, Tom looked through one bleary eye and said, "I would not drink it if I were you, Weasel. It will be the death of you."

It hurt to laugh. They had laughed so much the night before that Weasel's ribs ached. But he didn't heed the warning and muscled down a gulp against Tom's better judgment.

"Not too bad, Thomas." proclaimed Weasel with a cough. Len laughed while Weasel and Tom groaned in laughter, holding their ribs.

"Heidi and Maria are on their way here to pick you up. You are not to take the train home."

Tom and Weasel looked at each other shamefully.

"That's right! And yes, I did ring them so they wouldn't worry. They are aware of your raucous evening, or at least the major high-lights. I suggest that the two of you sleep this off and clean yourselves up before they arrive." Len tipped his hat. "You may keep the coffee, courtesy of the Livingstone Police," he said with a snicker and left the verandah to return to the police station.

"We aren't as young as we used to be, Weasel," admitted Tom rubbing his forehead.

"That's God's honest truth, my friend. This will set me back a few days, to be sure," said Weasel, downing another gulp of coffee and wincing.

Maria and Heidi arrived in Livingstone late that afternoon, but before heading to the Northwestern, they stopped in at the house where John was staying in the hopes of a visit with the young man. To their disappointment, the proprietor said that he had been away for a few days, and she didn't expect him back until later in the week. Maria assured a disappointed Heidi that they would try again soon now that Heidi was in on her secret.

When they got to the Northwestern, they found Tom and Weasel sitting on the verandah, uncharacteristically drinking coca colas, humbly awaiting their arrival and subsequent scolding.

"A fine pair the two of you are." started Heidi

"I wonder how much of the whole truth Leonard actually shared? added Maria

"Damn right, Maria!" Heidi affirmed, crossing her arms across her chest.

Tom knew better than to fight. They had lost this battle and any moral high ground. Weasel has also seen the worst of Maria's temper and has no desire to stoke it.

"We were wrong. We let the whisky get the best of us. And we are sorry that you felt you had to come all this way to collect us."

"That's right," added Weasel. "We meant no harm, and you both know how two old friends can get a bit carried away when they haven't seen each other for a while."

"I'd say, Uncle Weasel. You should be ashamed…the both of you!" stated Heidi unsympathetically.

"You could have fallen over into the boiling pot, Thomas! What were you thinking?" spat Maria with angry tears calling to memory their jaunt by the Falls the night previous.

"I am sorry Maria…and Heidi. It was foolish antics," said Tom, sincerely grabbing Maria's hand for forgiveness and throwing Heidi a look of endearment.

"At least we didn't die. And we still had fun with a couple of old blokes. So, I say we should stop all the sulking and just go on back home to Demberra. I, for one, am in no state to journey home to Katimo Mulilo tonight." said Weasel wearily, and they all couldn't help but laugh.

CHAPTER 2

JOHN SIDDLEY

"**M**ajor Warren T. Siddley (Retired) 9525, Fife Avenue, Salisbury, Southern Rhodesia" John Siddley stared at the business card he had pushed across Israel Bernstein's desk. The little Jewish man had a jovial disposition, a talkative type, thought John. The type of man that had all the secrets of this town catalogued.

John had been patient since his return to Livingstone three months ago. He had kept his continued relationship with Bradley quiet and had taken a clerk position at the Livingstone bank. Since the awful incident with the cattle a year and a half ago, he had been forced to return to Salisbury and live with the Major for over a year, who never let him out of his sight. He also dutifully returned to England with his father over the holidays for a visit with relatives in Spain and rang in the new year, 1932, like a dutiful son by his side.

The Major had always tried to do the right thing by him. He admittedly had not been the easiest child, yet the Major had stood by him through thick and thin, and John loved him for that. He had effectively been able to pass the cattle incident off as sheer stupidity and youthful ignorance, and his father had accepted that without question. But John felt he just couldn't tell him why he really had to return to Livingstone. If his father knew about Tom Sutton, he would never agree to any retribution or vengeance after all these years. He had become too soft in his latter middle age, thought John. But nonetheless, he didn't want his father to worry sick about his welfare, so with a great deal of convincing, he had finally received the Major's blessing to return, under the condition that he secure a job, avoid criminal elements, and come home to visit every other month.

Now back in Livingstone, John had to tread lightly. He knew that Maria, Tom's wife, for lack of a better description, had an eagle eye on him, and he was sure that she was still in communication with his father. It was her, after all, that had alerted the Major to the cattle incident in the first place, which had forced him home. In retrospect, it had probably been for the best and had allowed John to recuperate from his injuries in the luxury of his father's home.

He was sure that Maria thought of him as a reckless and mis-guided youth, that she alone could save him from self- destruction, and he knew she meant well. She had, after all, become his clos-est friend, maybe his only friend. Maria was several years older than him and not his type romantically, but she was undeniably attractive, warm, and genuinely kind.

He couldn't deny that he had enjoyed her company over the past couple of months. Why she chose to be with a man the like of Sutton, he did not understand. He also hated himself for using their friendship to track Tom's whereabouts and dig into his relationship with his ward and the locals. He only hoped that someday she, too, would know the awful truth about him and leave the man for her own sake. She deserved so much more.

"As you mentioned on the telephone, your father intends on buying property here?" inquired Issy offering John a cigar. John declined, but he removed his cap and took a seat across the desk.

"I thought I should at least make your acquaintance, Mr. Berry, and learn a bit more about this area. You do seem to be a mainstay around here," said John, attempting to sound casual.

"I have seen you at the bank a few times, isn't that right?"

"Yes. I arrived here about three months ago," stated John matter-of-factly. There was no need for Issy to know that he had been there before.

Issy lit his cigar and took a long pull releasing a cloud of smoke that hovered over his desk. John coughed.

"Oh, sorry, they are quite strong. Thomas Sutton, the man who owns Demberra over by Kabi Siding, always presents me with a box of these for Hanukah each year. Where the man gets these from is a mystery to me; Cubans, you know. Always very generous that Tom Sutton."

"I've heard of him," stated John nonchalantly.

"To be honest, if your father wants to buy land here, that's the man he should talk to. He has been very successful against stacked odds." beamed Issy with pride.

This was much easier than John had expected. The only reason he was here in Issy Berry's office was to extract information on Thomas Sutton, and he hadn't even needed an entrée. With a little further prodding and a flash of his youthful inquisitive green eyes, Issy was telling him Tom's entire life story. He had been a freedom fighter in Ireland and had moved to Africa to start a new life. He had a lovely adopted daughter Heidi, and a kind and beautiful partner in Maria. Although they weren't married, the arrangement seemed to suit them, Issy clarified. Mr. Sutton was well-liked by all the locals. He was a generous, hardworking, and shrewd businessman.

John did everything in his power to plaster a smile on his face and manufacture a look of wonder and endearment for this glowing biography of his father. Tom Sutton was seemingly infallible, and his life had apparently been one great success after another. All those years that Tom Sutton had been building this wonderful life and reputation for himself, John had been struggling with the memory he had left behind.

John's father, the Major, had kept his promise to the Irish priest Father Ryan all those years ago and had raised John, or Sean as he had remembered being called by his mother. He had been given an exemplary education in Hertfordshire, including trips overseas and all the trimmings of an upper-middle-class English childhood.

John had never been an easy child. The trauma he had suffered as a young boy had given him nightmares for years. He was a lonely child and had always had a difficult time making friends. Despite his generally subdued demeanor, he had a quick temper that flared up when he felt threatened. The Major, who never married, thought it best that John releases the memory of his father altogether if he was ever going to live a normal life. So, he reinforced the story that Tom had abandoned his son for a better life and would never be found in the hopes that the child would bond with him and let the memory of his father go. Unfortunately, this only embittered John and further fueled his hate for his biological father and his desire to find him and avenge his mother's death and his abandonment.

By nine, he was constantly begging the Major to help him search. And to appease the boy and keep his commitment to the priest, his father placed an advertisement for the long-lost Irishman, Thomas Sutton, in the New York Times every few months to no avail. Eventually, the Major sent John off to boarding school when he was twelve in the hopes that forced socialization and regimented discipline might prove beneficial, and it worked for a time.

At boarding school, John could no longer spend hours brooding over the past and his father. Like most teenagers, he eventually set aside his obsession in favor of sports, music, and girls. He even made some friends and had the opportunity to travel to France and Spain, which he found liberating. After high school concluded with his A levels, he began to contemplate his future, and the old wound gnawed at him again. Now a young man of seventeen, he felt he was old enough now to travel to America himself and find his father once and for all.

A fateful chance meeting at a London Garden party in the summer of 1930 changed everything for John. With John out of school, and the major nearing retirement age, the Major had been contemplating a Civil Servant position on the African continent. The position was short-term and came with a hefty pension at the end of it. He thought the adventure would be good for them both. John was obviously not initially thrilled by the idea and planned to tell the Major of his plans to go to America instead at the end of the summer. To make his father as pliant as possible, he had agreed to attend dozens of these boring government and military parties to show the Major that he was mature enough and worldly enough for the undertaking.

At these parties, they rubbed shoulders with important dignitaries and heads of state and exchanged pleasantries with some of the colonial affiliates. At one soiree in early July, while nursing an Old Fashioned alone at the bar, while his father worked the room, he overheard two names he hadn't heard spoken in nearly a decade in the same sentence "Weasel and Sutton." He whipped around in his seat to catch the exchange. A rotund police chief from a town near Victoria Falls in Rhodesia and some British government officials from the Cape were having a chin wag about a pair of Irishmen who had apparently settled not too far from the Falls.

"Uncle Weasel?" mouthed John to himself. "He's alive, and they're together."

"I'm sure he was part of the underground, you know", said the police officer. "Both of them-not that I care. None of my business out there in Africa, you know. Nice chap, Tom Sutton, all the same. Does love a good whisky."

"Don't all the Irish?" laughed the other man.

John was convinced. It was Weasel Byrne and Thomas Sutton, his father. The same Thomas Sutton who'd left him and his mother to die. And he was going to find him or die trying.

John, of course, never divulged this new information to his father but suddenly became exuberant about moving to Southern Rhodesia, which sealed the deal for the Major. John then convinced his father that after they were settled in Salisbury, he would like to see some of the continent, especially the Falls. The Major was delighted and gladly gave his blessing, happy to see that his son was finally letting go of the past and embracing this new opportunity.

Issy was still rambling on about Tom's days in the mines, his inheritance of Demberra, Heidi Van Wyk, his steadfastness to the land and business acumen, and so on. He never mentioned Grace or a son called Sean. They did not exist in the portrait of the man Issy knew, at least, that is what John understood from Issy's speech. When John had all the information he had come for, he abruptly stopped the man in mid-sentence.

"Pardon me. I thank you, Mr. Berry, for sharing all this information with me about Demberra and Mr. Sutton. He sounds like … quite the man. You've certainly shown me just how much potential this place has, should my father wish to purchase land here at some point in the future, or perhaps even myself."

"Young man, all I can say is that if you had a portion of the work ethic, shrewdness, and generosity of my dear friend Tom Sutton, you would have success here. It could be the ideal location to invest in property and settle down." smiled Issy, happy to recount Tom's story and set himself up as the real estate liaison.

"Yes indeed," said John, his eyes devoid of the same friendliness he had exhibited before. He abruptly rose and offered his hand to Issy, who, somewhat flustered, took the gesture and stood as well to shake his hand.

"Well then, I will contact you when I come across something suitable, Mr. Siddley, or shall I simply contact your father?" suggested Issy picking up the card from his desk.

"I only mentioned he might be interested, Mr. Berry. I will be in touch. Good day!"

John gave the confused man a firm handshake and departed his office before Issy could utter another word. There was something oddly familiar about this young man, but Issy just couldn't put his finger on it.

John climbed up the escape stairs to the second-floor bedroom at the back of Mrs. Papadopoulos' house, far from stellar accommodations provided to him courtesy of Bradley. But luxury wasn't why he was here, and this was good enough, a bed, a nightstand, and a hallway bathroom. John was grateful that the woman understood little English, which saved him a lot of unnecessary conversations.

The bed groaned as John flopped onto it, and he kicked off his shoes. He lay there for a while staring at the peeling ceiling paint. The electric globe hung above him like the scorching Livingstone sun. His uninviting warm bottle of beer sat beside him. He pulled a cigarette and matchbox from his pocket and, lighting the cigarette, exhaled, releasing his tension along with a perfect ring of smoke. The sun was beginning to set outside, and soon, the moon would illuminate the room. He was more than comfortable just lying here on this bed and staring at the ceiling.

He was still obviously committed to making Tom Sutton pay for what he had done to him and his mother, but he couldn't deny that he was puzzled by the portrait of the man Issy described. Was he really so generous and well-liked, or was Issy just a poor, manipulated little man like Bradley had suggested? John wondered if he might get even closer to Tom's inner circle, maybe through Maria. He would never hurt her personally, of course. He believed her to be a victim in the relationship. But maybe he could get to Tom Sutton through his ward, which he seemed to dote on.

John's thoughts were interrupted by a knock and an undeniable raspy voice with a thick Greek accent.

"John, you in there?" Max croaked.

John sat up in bed as the door opened, and Max's face came into view, John narrowed his eyes at him.

"What do you want?"

"Came to pick you up. We have a job to do."

"What job?"

"Some man just arrived in Livingstone. Owes him money. We have to retrieve it."

"Tell Mr. Bradley I'm not interested. He should know that I only involve myself with work concerning one man and one man only," responded John dismissively.

"Who, Sutton. I thought you would have had enough after the cattle. Why do you hate him so much, eh?" Max inquired.

"None of your business, Max."

"I know…You're after the same thing as Mr. Bradley. What's buried there at Demberra."

"Buried?"

"Don't pretend, John. Max is not as stupid as you think. Why don't you and I strike a deal?"

John decided to play along, curious about this new development. "Go on."

"I am asking you to be my partner, John." Max huffed with exasperation.

"On one condition. Now that you know what I'm after, you are going to have to assure me that we are in this together 50/50, and Bradley knows nothing about it."

Max nodded eagerly.

"Alright, tell me what you know and how you think we should proceed because Bradley has told me a great deal... This way, I can see if our information matches, and then I'll judge whether I can trust you or not." lied John.

John offered his would be partner Max a warm beer, and for the next half an hour, Max told John everything he knew. He elaborated on Bradley's connection to the old man Mamba. Apparently, Sutton had stolen gold coins from the old man that rightfully belonged to Bradley and buried the box under his verandah. And there was a secret entrance in the house to get to them, Hansie had said. When the old African reported the theft to the authorities, Sutton gave them Bradley's name as a suspect. Since then, Sutton had been a thorn in Bradley's side for obvious reasons. This must be why Bradley had tried to swindle Sutton out of his property, not just for revenge but for his coins. It all made sense. John nodded in agreement as if he was simply verifying Max's version of the story against his own.

"That's exactly it! Well done, Max," said John beaming, and they clinked bottles.

"Hurry up, partner. We don't have all day, do we? Have to get big boss his money."

The men clinked one more time and gulped down the last of their celebratory beers, and left Max's mother's house.

CHAPTER 3

RECONNAISSANCE

Demberra was full of life. The weather was ideal, and the farm was free once again to grow and expand. Tom had already begun work on the adjoining King property, and now with Weasel in tow, it didn't seem like work at all as the two chatted and laughed their way through the days. Weasel had been at Demberra for almost a week and was bemoaning his need to return to his trading post daily. All had long since been forgiven between Weasel and Maria, and they fell back into their old endearing patterns of bickering.

Even though Heidi hadn't been privy to some of the history the others had shared, she caught up quickly. And despite her youth, she had been able to hold her own with these two men for most of her life already. With the addition of Maria, they were quite a foursome.

The company was the best kind, the easy kind. Where no one had to put on pretenses or civilities, this made for a week of entertaining evenings that never ended before midnight and included raucous conversations and cocktails by the open fire.

It was Sunday evening, and they had all retreated to the verandah after dinner for coffee, continuing their dinner debate on the current affairs in Europe.

"Let me tell you, Tom, another world war is in the making. The Depression in Europe will lead to it," Weasel said with emphatic hand gestures, an indication that he had had too much wine at dinner.

"What do you even know of Europe, Uncle Weasel? You haven't been there in ages." snapped Heidi, and they all laughed loudly at Weasel's expense.

Somewhere in the dark beyond the pagoda that now cradled heavy bougainvillea came the sound of a car engine. The frivolity stopped instantly, and Tom rose and walked to the edge of the verandah and called out.

"Here I was about to dazzle everyone with the source of my knowledge," said Weasel wounded.

"Shh," whispered Maria

On the road below, Tom was blinded by two headlights. "Turn off the damn headlights, man."

The headlights dimmed instantly, and the engine shut off. As Tom approached the car, a man called out.

"Pardon me for intruding like this, Mr. Sutton. My vehicle ran out of fuel on my drive back from Lusaka. Would you be kind enough to spare me some?" the man apologized sheepishly.

Tom creased his forehead in recognition. He had seen this young man before.

"Pardon me, sir. I'm John. You rescued me two summers ago from the bush."

"Yes, of course! The young cattle thief!" said Tom with satisfaction.

"Come on up to the verandah and meet everyone, John."

"Oh no, it's alright, Mr. Sutton. I do not wish to interrupt your family time."

"Nonsense, my boy," Tom chuckled and grabbed John by the elbow.

"We have a visitor, everyone." Tom bellowed as Maria, Weasel, and Heidi all waited at the edge of the verandah to get a look at the wayward traveler.

As soon as John reached the light of the verandah, Maria knew who it was instantly and tempered her impulse to welcome him with open arms. She hadn't seen him since before Christmas. She was anxious that John might falter, but he did not and instantly avoided her gaze.

"John, allow me to introduce you to everyone. This is my old friend Timothy Byrne." John barely gave Weasel eye contact for fear that he would recognize him, but no apparent recognition flooded his expression."

"How do you do," said Weasel standing only long enough for introductions and then slumping back into his chair.

"This is Maria," Tom said, gesturing to Maria, who politely offered her hand.

"Yes, of course, Mrs. Sutton, I remember you well, madam. I can't thank you enough for everything you did for me… back in the bush."

Tom did not correct John's assumption but moved on to Heidi.

"My ward, Heidi," said Tom as Heidi extended her hand and stared at him with wide blue eyes like a child, unmoving until a wave of a blush crept up her neck, and she released her hand and dropped her gaze.

He was definitely handsome, Heidi mused. He was a little shorter than Tom, with a lean athletic build. His hair was dark and thick, and she suspected that if it wasn't slicked to his head, it might be wild and unruly. His skin was fair and tinged slightly red from the African sun. And his eyes, as they held her gaze for a moment, were green like the sea in Paloma when the sun struck it a certain way. When she felt her cheeks redden, she was certain that he noticed.

"Stay for a refreshment John." urged Maria

"A coffee would be dandy, Mrs. Sutton," answered John, feeling like he was on display.

"Coffee, after making a trip down these dusty roads. I insist you have something a little stronger and colder."

"Well, a beer, if I may?" said John politely

Jonas arrived as if on cue, or maybe Maria had skipped out to summon him.

"An Irish for me," announced Weasel as soon as Jonas arrived.

"Well, I suppose it would be impolite of me not to join these two fine gentlemen. Jonas, make it two Irish, one beer, and two sherries for the ladies."

Tom ushered John to the seat next to him, and they all sat down. The women were opposite them, with Weasel in between. This was only the second time he had been in his father's presence as a young man. The first time he had been barely conscious. Looking at him now, he seemed like a conjuring man from his dreams. Tom looked the same to him, with just a bit of grey on the temples and a few wrinkles around the eyes. He was just as jovial as he remembered but also a little worn in a way he couldn't quite describe. He wanted to like him, but how could he?

"I had heard a lot about your ward from Mr. Bradley, sir. But I had no idea she was so beautiful, Mr. Sutton," said John coolly as he looked directly at Heidi once again, locking eyes with her.

"Let me warn you of one thing, boy. In my house, we do not mention Bradley's name, let alone what he thinks of Heidi. Don't tell me you still work for that piece of…?" Maria threw Tom a look across the table. "Er…man?"

John flushed slightly at the mention of his employer. He was tethering rough waters, but he recovered quickly.

"Absolutely not, sir," John said stoically. "Not after what happened. I'm sorry, I meant no disrespect."

"The man is a scoundrel. He robbed my farm manager, Simalala's father Mamba, of his life savings, amongst other atrocities that I won't speak of in front of ladies. And he's a stone- cold liar."

What a hypocrite, thought John, coming from a man whose whole life had been built on lies. John had no great love for Bradley, but in his mind, Tom was no better. Bradley had sent him and the others to confiscate that old African man's cattle to prevent him from selling them to Tom, which he hadn't been proud about. But it was retribution, that's what Bradley had told him. Sutton had been even sneakier. He had earned the old man's trust and then stolen the gold right from under his nose and tried to frame Bradley in the process. Max's story made sense. And the gold must be buried here at Demberra, right under where they sat.

And if it belonged to Bradley to begin with, as Max had suggested, then the old man deserved what he got. As far as John was concerned, he felt no moral obligation to the Africans anyway after his assault in the bush. All John had to do was to get Tom Sutton to trust him, and then he would help Bradley get his gold back and bring down Sutton in the process. John smiled at Maria to make sure she was buying his sincerity. The last thing he needed was another letter to his father.

"That shrewd old Barotse man." piped up Weasel, who had been nursing his whisky and watching the volley play out without interrupting. "I always knew he kept tins of the silver coins for trading, but I never knew about the box of gold half-sovereigns.

"That's because it happened before we arrived in Africa, Weasel, years ago."

"What a bastard that Bradley is, I never liked him. Sorry ladies" added Weasel

"Just the mention of his name makes me want to punch something." snarled Tom

Tom clenched his jaw, and for an instant, John was looking at his mirror image. Not that the father and son bore much, if any, resemblance. Now that he was grown, John saw that he clearly favored his mother's side of the family. But Tom's mannerisms were so familiar to him because they were also his. He suddenly became afraid that they would all figure him out, so he channeled all his focus into making sure he did not unconsciously mimic the gestures or postures of the man beside him.

Well, that was rich, he thought. He couldn't believe what a liar his father was. Even Weasel had bought this ruse that the theft had happened before they arrived in Livingstone. What a lark!

But they had always been partners, and it did seem odd that Sutton would have acted alone without Weasel's knowledge. But maybe he was just too greedy to share. Anyway, Maria must also be in the dark about it too. Perhaps Sutton would simply kick her out when he'd had enough of her. Being across the table from Weasel wasn't easy for John either. He retained some vague memories of his Uncle Weasel from his childhood. He had always been silly with him, quick with a joke, and eager to entertain his childish folly. Was he as much to blame as his father for leaving Ireland, or was it all Tom's idea? He liked to believe it was the latter. Could he find room in his heart to forgive Weasel? At moments that evening, he felt Weasel's eye lingering on him longer than normal. Did he see something? Did he remember him? If he did, he said nothing.

"I hope you won't punch me, Mr. Sutton," Sean said, a poor attempt at humor, trying to lighten the mood and get off the topic of Bradley.

Tom laughed, and then everyone laughed. That was the end of the interrogation. Tom's temper had always been hot but quick. When it subsided, he easily moved on without hindrance. From then on, the five of them became engrossed in various conversations that segued naturally from topic to topic. Weasel wanted validation of his theories on an impending war, and John, having been in Europe the year before, corroborated everyone's worst fears.

John had long since lost any semblance of an Irish accent but nonetheless was careful not to make any mention of Ireland and presented himself flawlessly as the product of an English Prep School, with lots of tales to tell to bolster it. The bottomless drinks also lowered everyone's social awkwardness, including Heidi, who, after three Sherries, became her usual animated self, entertaining them all with stories from her recent student teaching experience. She even caught John staring at her a few times, and this time she didn't look away.

"What's your surname again, lad?" asked Weasel late into the evening. "I'm not sure you ever mentioned it."

John couldn't lie because Maria already knew what it was. He only hoped that the Irishman wouldn't make any connection. "It's Siddley," said John gingerly.

"Sounds familiar, doesn't it, Tom? Wasn't there a Siddley based in Dublin during the uprising?"

"Yes, I do believe so- a major if I recall correctly," said Tom scrutinizing John more closely.

"Oh no, my father was never stationed in Ireland. I have lived my whole life in Hertfordshire." stuttered John, trying to reel them back from the rabbit hole that they were staring into. "He's always been a very doting father. In fact, if he had ever known about the cattle incident, I'm not sure he would have forgiven me." Maria and Heidi exchanged looks, aware of the letter Maria had sent to the major. "Besides, Siddley is a very common name in England."

That seemed to satisfy the Irishmen's inquiry, at least for the time being. Besides, they were too inebriated at this point to argue further. John suddenly glanced at his watch; it was past eleven. He had not meant to stay this long or have this good of a time. He was supposed to be here on a reconnaissance mission, but he had had an undeniably enjoyable evening despite himself. He had to get out of here before he softened any further, he thought.

"Petrol, Mr. Sutton?" John asked abruptly as he stood and pushed into his chair.

"What? Don't be foolish, boy. It's too late, anyway. The whole farm's asleep, and I can barely walk in a straight line, let alone go and pump petrol for you. You'll stay here at Demberra tonight. Maria, would you be kind enough to show our guest to one of the guest rooms?

Maria smiled and, nodding, gestured that John should follow her.

"That is very kind. Goodnight, Mr. Sutton, Mr. Byrne, and Miss Sutton." John said, allowing his eyes to linger a few seconds longer on Heidi as he rounded the corner with Maria into the house.

"I'm off too," stated Tom emphatically with a pat on the table, stopping only to peck Heidi on the cheek on his way to his bedroom.

"I suppose it's just the die-hards, Uncle Weasel." laughed Heidi,

"Actually, my dear, I think a bed would be delightful right about now. I can't lie," said Weasel sleepily.

"To be honest, uncle, me too," said Heidi, and they both left the verandah and turned in for the night.

Outside the guest room, John spoke quietly.

"Maria, I'm really sorry. I didn't mean to intrude like this."

"Not a bother at all, John. I'm glad you're here. You know I tried to stop in and see you about a week ago, but you weren't there."

"Oh yes, a friend from out of town was arriving, and I had to meet him in Bulawayo." John hated lying to her, but he had come so far already.

"Ah, well, I'm glad you're here now. I wanted you to meet Heidi anyway. I thought you might have some things in common."

"Thank you again for your hospitality," said John coldly, not wishing to discuss Heidi. "I think I will turn it in now."

As Maria walked back to her bedroom, she wondered what chord she had struck to cause John to be so dismissive. She was glad that he stayed. She hadn't liked skulking around behind Tom's back, and she knew that she had not imagined the glances being thrown between Heidi and John all evening. But something was off. Maybe things would be clearer in the light of day.

CHAPTER 4

HAPPY COINCIDENCES

John found Tom sipping his morning coffee on the verandah. He, too, was an early riser and had hoped to get Tom alone. He was here to gather as many details as possible, and that would be easier without Weasel's lingering gaze or the women to distract him.

"Good morning, lad," said Tom as John emerged from the house.

"Thank you again for your hospitality, Mr. Sutton."

"Please, it's Tom, just call me Tom. How old are you anyway, boy?"

"Twenty, sir," said John taking the seat next to him.

"Not too much older than Heidi, then?" stated Tom. "Cup of coffee?"

"Yes, please, sir."

"There's a pot on the sideboard back there, help yourself."

"I couldn't help but notice you gawking at my Heidi last night."

John was caught off guard but took his time crafting a response as he poured his coffee. "Really? I thought I was being subtle, and maybe I thought you were too drunk to notice."

"An Irishman always sleeps with one open eye, son, especially when it comes to his daughter, liquor or no liquor. Heidi is a good girl, and I'll accept nothing but the utmost respect deserving of a young lady, understood?"

"Tom, you have my intentions all wrong." stuttered John, being thrown off his game slightly. Besides, sir, I know you would kill me."

"You can bet on it," said Tom without giving him eye contact and taking another swig of his coffee.

"I would never take advantage of your kindness, Tom. Not ever," said John, laying it on a little thick.

"Then why did you lie to me, John?" Tom turned to face him and stared at him, unmoving.

"Lie?" John's palms turned sweaty at the accusation. What was the man getting at? Did he know why he was here? How could he know? Maria hadn't let on that anything was amiss, had she?

Tom continued, "Just cut the act, boy. I've been around the block too many times. I can smell deception when I see it."

"I…I don't understand, Mr. Sutton, sir. I told you I was out of petrol when I arrived last night. Your house was simply on my route home to Livingstone."

"Rather odd because I put one hand on the bonnet of your car last night, my hand should have been hot to the touch if you had been travelling all the way from Lusaka as you so claimed. And your tires are hardly worse for the wear. So, my guess is that this little trip was planned and that you drove here yesterday morning and were resting at the outpost twenty minutes from here. This whole thing was orchestrated, so you could make sure your car had just enough petrol to get you here, and that's all."

John couldn't help his mouth from hanging open for a split second before the cogs in his brain quickly mechanized and churned out a viable explanation. He already assumed that he was keen on Heidi, and that seemed like the most believable excuse and one he might believe.

"Well, I must say you have an amazing sense of judgment, Tom. You're right, and I did plan to stop here on purpose. I had no real reason to come, and to be honest, I wasn't sure how you would receive me after the cattle incident. But I had to find a way to see her."

"Who?" Tom asked "Heidi, of course, sir."

"Have the two of you met before?" questioned Tom.

"What? Oh no, sir! I saw her in Livingstone with Mrs. Sutton about a week ago, from a distance, and I just had to meet her, which is why I put on the petrol fiasco." John knew that Heidi and Maria had tried to see him when they were last in Livingstone, so the timing was plausible enough, John thought.

Tom paused and scrutinized the young man before responding. What other reason would a young fellow come here to Demberra. It was completely logical that he would have an interest in Heidi. She was a very pretty girl, and there weren't too many attractive and eligible young women with her background and education in these parts. And there was something about this young man's eyes that softened him. Something about him seemed so familiar, so reassuring.

"I suppose I would have pulled the same stupid antics at your age for the sake of a girl. Now your mind that she is not just any girl. She is special, and it will be me you reckon with if her heart gets broken."

"Yes, of course, sir. I would never…." John stammered, happy that Tom had bought his ruse. Or was it a ruse? He was here to gather details that would inevitably sabotage Tom Sutton, but he couldn't deny that he was attracted to Heidi. He shrugged off his weakness. She was only a tool to be used in Tom's destruction, and he reminded himself. She had replaced him, and Tom Sutton hadn't thought twice about forgetting him and choosing this girl to be his new daughter. He hated her too.

"Now that the lecture is over, what say you and I saddle up the horses, and I show you around a bit before breakfast," said Tom rising and returning his coffee cup to the sideboard and grabbing his hat.

John couldn't believe his luck. "Yes, yes, Tom, that would be wonderful."

It felt odd tacking up Soleil for anyone other than Heidi or Maria, but horseback was the best way to tour the farm, and it was a perfect morning for riding.

"You ride?" asked Tom

"Yes, yes, of course," responded John, accepting Soleil's reins. "I'm sure Heidi won't mind."

Tom was proud of everything he had accomplished at Demberra. John knew little of the arduous undertaking the ranch had been and only saw the wealth and prosperity it now enjoyed. He was jealous and angry at Tom's good fortune, considering his humble past. Tom wasn't aware of the animosity and proudly explained the workings of the farm, from the fireguards to the cattle dipping. They toured the fields and crops as Tom expounded on all the advances he had made and successes they had had. His excitement was only perceived as boastfulness by John, but he smiled and nodded as they made their way back to the stables.

They washed their hands with an outdoor spigot and knocked the dirt off their boots. "Rub them down well, Simon," Tom yelled over his shoulder to the stable hand as they walked back to the house. "Yes, Bwana," came the reply.

"Come on, John, let's have some breakfast, and I'll bet your stomach is grumbling by now."

"No, thank you, Tom. I don't mean to be more of a bother."

"Ridiculous! Besides, Maria seems to like having a new visitor here, and she will be offended if you don't partake in one of her renowned breakfast feasts."

How little he knew about Maria, thought John, as he nodded and followed Tom up to the house. They discovered them all in the dining room, awaiting breakfast and chattering pleasantly. Maria sat at one head of the table with Weasel and Heidi on either side. She smiled warmly at John as they entered. Weasel was nursing his third cup of black coffee, whining about his head. Tom greeted everyone and took his seat opposite Maria at the other head of the table.

"Good morning, Mrs. Sutton, Mr. Byrne, Miss. Sutton" said John politely, still standing, trying to decide whether it would be more advantageous to sit next to Heidi and be forced to face Weasel in the light of day or if he should sit next to Weasel instead and continue to play up the romance between himself and Heidi across the table. He chose the latter.

"Dear God, my head. Jaysus!" wailed Weasel as the ladies snickered. "What was all the shenanigans this morning. You lot are a bloody noisy bunch at six a.m.

"It is a farm Weasel," stated Maria unapologetically. "We all get up quite early around here."

"Oh, Miss Sutton. I had the pleasure of riding your filly this morning with your father, I mean Uncle, around the farm. I would like to express my gratitude for lending her to me. She is indeed a darling."

Heidi blushed at the compliment. Why must she be so disarming, thought John. He wondered how she must have been as a child when she first met Tom Sutton. She looked radiant again today, in a light green dress, with little pearl buttons at the neckline. Her eyes were a brighter blue than he remembered from the night before, and she smiled easily. He couldn't allow himself to have any real feelings for this girl. She was just a pawn in this game and only that. She wasn't going to stand in the way of his plan. He swiftly broke eye contact with her and returned to a conversation of pleasantries for the remainder of breakfast, avoiding her gaze at all costs.

Weasel knew he had to get back to his trading post. This could not become an extended vacation, as much as he enjoyed the company.

"Heidi, now that you're finished with school and all that, why don't you come up and spend some time with your Uncle Weasel at my outpost," suggested Weasel gingerly as Tom's eyes narrowed on him.

"Now, now, Thomas, she is, after all, a young woman and not a child anymore. She has managed to live alone in Salisbury without an incident, right? And she'll be with me the whole time, and I won't let her out of my sight. Besides, I could use the company and a hand in the shop, just for a week or two. I have a shipment of new furniture and housewares coming from the States next week, and Heidi would be such a help organizing it."

"Oh, please, Uncle Tom," begged Heidi, forgetting that John was at the table and reverting to a childlike plea. "I've never been, and you always promised me that we would go someday. Besides, I'm sure Uncle Weasel will take me fishing, too, right Uncle Weasel? … and I could be of help, couldn't I." she and Weasel exchanged winks across the table.

"Maria? How about you. Can you manage without Heidi around?" Tom asked, hoping for an ally.

"Thomas, don't be silly. I have lots of help here. Let the girl go and have some fun-you're only young once." Maria implored.

"I really need to get on the road today, and we've already missed the train. John, aren't you headed back to Livingstone? Do you think you could drive us?

"I'll drive you right to the boat if you like." offered John, still not acknowledging Heidi, but for a fleeting glance.

Heidi, tickled with excitement, abruptly excused herself to pack for the getaway. When Maria found her in her room after breakfast, her suitcase lay on the bed brimming with clothes, with more scattered on the floor around her. She looked utterly distraught as she rummaged through her closet fitfully.

"You've never been to Katimo Mulilo Heidi, have you?"

"Why do you ask?"

"Just asking. I used to work for Timothy there, and that is where I met your father, Uncle Thomas, I mean."

"I know," said Heidi, distracted.

"Well, all this time, you never asked, that's all."

"About what?" said Heidi trying to wedge a pair of shoes into the corner of her already overstuffed suitcase.

"Did you ever wonder about your Uncle Weasel and me," said Maria, gently sitting on the side of her bed.

"Well, of course, I did. I mean, I assumed that you…." said Heidi pushing the suitcase aside and coming to sit beside her on the bed.

"We weren't…lovers," Maria said seriously. "Maria, you don't owe me any explanations."

"But I want you to know that your Uncle Thomas was my first and my only. I just don't want you to think less of me." Maria began to cry softly.

"Oh Maria, I could never think less of you, even if he wasn't. But the fact that you have been so true to Tom makes me angry. You deserve more. He should do the decent thing and make you his wife. That's what you want, isn't it?"

"Of course!" said Maria through sobs.

"Let me talk some sense into him, please." implored Heidi stroking her hair.

"No, no! He must not feel forced into this. And I don't want him just to marry me because he feels sorry for me."

"Oh Maria, you know he loves you. I, for one, know he loves you more than anything. This is all about his past and has nothing to do with you. But I won't betray your confidence if that's what you want." Heidi said, comforting her. "But if you ever change your mind, I'm happy to speak to him. You are an amazing woman Maria Gomes, and I, for one, believe you are perfect for Thomas Sutton. You will always have my blessing for what it's worth."

Maria and Heidi embraced in a tangle of hair and wet cheeks for a few minutes. Maria felt better, and so did Heidi, although she wished that Maria would allow her to speak reason to her uncle.

"You will always be like a little sister to me, Heidi. I love you so much."

"And I you. But right now, I think I need a mother to try and help me decide what to wear, especially now that John Siddley will be escorting us most of the way there," said Heidi with urgency and a laugh.

"I told you he was handsome, didn't I." beamed Maria. "…and I think he likes you."

"No, he does not," said Heidi coyly, undeniably glad for the affirmation.

Maria helped Heidi select her best clothing options designed solely to beguile and intrigue young men, and together they snapped the bulging case closed.

"Uncle Tom, could you please carry my case for me," Heidi yelled out into the hallway.

"I don't know why I bother having help when I do everything myself," Tom mumbled as he dutifully brought her case out to John's Buick waiting on the road and placed it in the trunk.

Heidi combed and sprayed her hair to give it a little extra bounce and tied a paisley green silk scarf around her head to protect her hair from the dust of the road. A swipe of bright red lipstick and a pair of chic blue-tinted round keyhole sunglasses completed the look. Standing in front of her mirror, Maria confessed that she could have been on the cover of a Hollywood magazine. Heidi humbly diverted the compliment.

"Be cautious of that young man, Heidi. I like him very much, but he has some skeletons in his closet," whispered Maria at the car door as she gave her kiss on the cheek goodbye.

"Don't worry, I intend to," she whispered back to her.

With Weasel in the passenger seat and Heidi tucked into the back seat of the convertible, filled with a full tank, the engine rumbled to a start, and they were off.

"Take care of her, Weasel," Tom called after them, and Weasel turned and gave him a mock salute.

"She'll be fine. You have to trust her, Thomas."

"Where do you suppose a boy of that age gets a car like that to drive around."

"Well certainly not from his boss at the bank, but I would suppose from his rich father," suggested Maria as they walked back up to the house.

"How did you know that he worked at the bank," asked Tom suspiciously

"Oh, he mentioned something about working at the Livingstone bank last night. Don't you remember?" said Maria recovering quickly.

"No, I missed that. I only heard about it this morning on the horse ride. And what were you and Heidi whispering about so secretly before she left anyway?" he inquired.

"Mind your own business, Thomas Sutton," she said with a smirk as she linked her arm to his.

"You two can't gang up on me."

"We already have," Maria said playfully, and as she bounced up the verandah stairs, he slapped her bottom playfully.

"I'll see you in the bedroom Mr. Sutton."

Will you now?" said Tom as he hurried up the stairs behind her, laughing, grateful in that moment to have Demberra to themselves.

CHAPTER 5

RECKLESS ABANDON

The drive from Demberra to Livingstone was gratefully pressure-free for John. Heidi and Weasel chattered most of the way about her adventures in Salisbury and what they would do at Katimo Mulilo, with a few asides from John here and there. It was clear to John that his Uncle Weasel had a history with Heidi and that she had come to look at him as the same fun-loving uncle he once had as a small boy. He couldn't help but feel jealous. He wanted to shake the little man and make him remember him.

The whipping wind had untamed John's dark wavy hair, and at one point, as Weasel stared into what were Grace's eyes, he muttered, "you remind me of someone" under his breath. But when Heidi questioned him, he abandoned the idea, muttering. "Ah, never mind, he just reminds me of someone I knew once, someone close to both your uncle Tom and me."

This was the first affirmation of his mother. Weasel must have been thinking of Grace, for John knew well that he had his mother's eyes, as evidenced by his mother's description and the old photograph Father Ryan had given him. The one he kept in his dresser drawer wrapped in priest's letters. There was also remorse in Weasel's tone, even regret maybe. John's resolve became a little shaken for the moment.

When the Buick merged onto the main street, it was five o'clock.

"Where do you intend to spend the night?" John asked them both.

"The Northwestern, where the beds are always soft, and the drinks are always ice cold." laughed Weasel, and Heidi giggled.

"The Northwestern it is then," said John trying to sound as charming as possible while checking the rear-view mirror for Heidi's reaction.

The car made a final left turn down the hill and stopped at the feet of the hotel's porch. Weasel jumped out and helped Heidi out of the back seat while John procured their bags from the trunk.

"Thank you for driving us here John…oh why don't you join us later for a drink?" said Weasel as he slammed the passenger car door.

"I would love to," he replied, climbing back into his seat.

"Thank you, John," said Heidi politely

"Goodbye, Heidi," John replied with a smile, then raised her temperature a couple of degrees. He was very attractive, especially with his hair all disheveled and hanging in his eyes, she thought. He also knew how to lay on the charm, thought Heidi. She was determined not to allow her feelings to get the best of her. After all, she knew nothing of this man except what Maria had told her. And even though Maria liked him, she was wary. So far, he had only shown poor judgment in his choice of company, no matter how nice he seemed or how handsome he was, he had a wealth to prove to win her over.

Back at his accommodation, John bathed, put on a crisp white cuffed shirt and slacks and applied a thick dollop of pomade to his unruly hair. As he ran his fingers through his thick mop, he smiled to himself as he remembered how much his mother liked to tousle his hair and how much he had hated it. She wouldn't have approved of this pomade at all. Before he left for the hotel, he had a couple of loose ends to attend to. According to his agreement with his father, he was due back in Salisbury in two weeks. Given the recent developments, that would not be possible. But he didn't need his father showing up here and putting a wrench in his plans. He had to get a letter in the post before five.

Dear Father,

How are you? I am keeping well here in Livingstone. I enjoy my work at the bank, and I have even started to travel a little to the surrounding villages and towns on the weekends. Please don't be concerned, and I am keeping out of trouble.

I am writing to you because I know I am due back in Salisbury in two weeks, as we agreed. However, I must beg that you excuse me for not making the trip this time.

I have met a girl. She is beautiful, well-educated, and witty. Her name is Heidi.

I want to bring her to Salisbury to meet you. But I suspect her father would not give her permission yet, as our courtship is so new.

I hope you can understand. I will write again soon. Your loving son,

John

He hated lying to his father, and in some ways, he wished the letter could be true and that his life was simpler. Carrying around this burden all these years was beginning to take its toll. Well, the letter was mostly true, he decided. He was working at the bank, and he had ventured out of Livingstone, albeit to spy on Tom Sutton. And he did believe all that he said about Heidi's good qualities. He knew the major would believe his story because, more than anything, his father feared that something would happen to him and John would be left alone in this world. The sooner he saw him married, the better.

He sealed the envelope, addressed the outside, and promised that he would tell him the truth when the time was right. He checked his watch as he locked his bedroom door. After the post office, he had just enough time for a stopover at Bradley's office before heading to the hotel.

He bounded up the stairs to Bradley's office two steps at a time and barged in unannounced, catching him by surprise.

"Did you ever hear of knocking?" he barked from his leather swivel chair. His blonde henchman Hansie was lounging at the desk that used to be occupied by his secretary. Bradley's reputation had made its way through all the female circles, and it was unlikely the man would ever fill that seat with a secretary again.

"I want to discuss something with you, Bradley," John said with authority.

"What, no more, Mr.?"

"You call me, Siddley, I call you Bradley. I think that's fair, don't you?"

Bradley turned to face Hansie and growled.

"Kick this brat out. I don't have time for the likes of him."

The blonde man cracked his knuckles and pulled himself from the chair.

"If he bloody touches me, I shall declare warfare on those gold sovereigns, Bradley."

Bradley instantly put up his hand and stopped Hansie in his tracks.

"Leave us alone, Hansie."

"You sure, boss?"

"Yes! I'm fine…just go."

With the order, Hansie narrowed his eyes at John as he left the office. John did not flinch, even though Hansie scared him.

"Please take a seat, Mr. Siddley? sneered Bradley with the typical smarmy charm he lathered on for clients and women.

"It appears the brat has officially hit a nerve," said John sarcastically, taking the seat opposite him.

"Oh, John, you aren't a brat. I jest, that's all. I am a businessman, and you know that. Perhaps, you are not as dangerous to me as you might perceive. It all depends on how much you know, dear chap."

"I'll cut to the chase Bradley. I spent last evening at Demberra, and I know all about the gold sovereigns hidden there. And now it is suddenly clear to me why Tom Sutton is a thorn in your side."

Bradley betrayed nothing.

"Sundowner?"

John accepted the glass of bourbon and waited, his heart nearly beating out of his chest. He wanted to strike a deal with Bradley and keep Max out of it. Bradley couldn't know he'd heard the story from him. If he could convince Bradley that he had heard it from Sutton himself, he could entrap him. He didn't care about the gold. He only wanted his father to suffer. And then, he would leave for Livingstone and put his past behind him.

"The coins are far more valuable than you can fathom, Priceless, I would say."

"I know," John said, playing along.

"You do know that if the information you harbor is hazardous to me, I could have you disappear without a trace." Bradley allowed the threat to linger in the room for a moment to gauge John's reaction. John wasn't sure what he meant but countered.

"That would be unwise. Before coming here today, I posted a letter to my father in Salisbury, and you know the major. And I informed him that I had run into you and that if anything nefarious happened to me in the foreseeable future, you would most certainly be the man responsible."

Bradley leaned back in his chair. He was ruffled, although he was good at covering it.

"Touché, but that was not necessary. I am not that reckless, John. I'm sure we can make this situation mutually beneficial, what do you say?"

"I think I could be amenable to that."

"I have only one condition. When the coins are retrieved, our deal is over, and you leave town."

"Fine," said John.

Bradley refilled their glasses and slid John's across the desk. They raised their glasses in mid-air without breaking eye contact.

"So, you've ingratiated yourself to Sutton, have you? Beware that mick is a cheat and a liar."

"He claimed you stole the money; can you believe it? When he himself hoodwinked that old African man. He even hid it from his friend Weasel. So, if the coins are under the verandah, how do we get into the house to retrieve them."

Trapped! Max had opened his big mouth just like he had expected, and this kid, out of some weird hatred for Sutton, had bought the whole story, hook, line, and sinker. John had no idea Bradley had orchestrated the hold thing, and Bradley didn't skip a beat.

"That bastard Irishman has managed to thwart all my efforts so far, as you know. But if you can get close to him and find out where he buried it exactly, I can plan how to destroy his whole operation. When Demberra is rightfully mine, we can divide up the spoils. And that includes the women."

Bradley, of course, knew exactly where the metal lunch box of gold coins was buried because he had buried it there himself nine years ago when he wasn't much older than John was now. He also knew that Sutton knew nothing of where it was hidden, how could he? So young John Siddley had been conspiring with Max. But it was good that John had heard Max's version of the tale first so that his new familiarity with Sutton wouldn't cloud his perception. He wondered if his father, the major, had perhaps had some sordid history with Sutton that the boy had concealed. He didn't care either way. He had John Siddley solidly in his pocket now.

If he could get to the boy to lure the Suttons away from Demberra for a few days, he could set the place on fire and destroy everything Tom Sutton had built. Sutton would then be forced to leave, and he could sweep up both properties for himself at a discount and finally retrieve his gold. John Siddley would serve as a tool in this operation and then would be dealt with accordingly, just like the Afrikaner and eventually Max too. When he had finished with him, the brat would be sorry he had ever set foot in Livingstone.

Watching Bradley smooth his mustache and gloat made John wonder who he hated more, William Bradley or Thomas Sutton. He detested everything about Bradley and was still ashamed of his involvement in the cattle incident last year, even though he had been mostly duped into it. He also despised the way he talked about Maria and Heidi. Maria had been a good friend to him when he needed one most. And though he didn't know Heidi well, no girl, especially one as sweet as her, deserved the filth that oozed from Bradley's lips.

On second thoughts, if he could find out where the coins were buried, he'd simply dig them up himself and report them both to the authorities. Then they would all be free of Tom Sutton and William Bradley. He began to feel a sudden rage pulsing through him. He was beginning to fantasize about them both rotting in jail together. But he restrained himself and manufactured a smile.

"You will have revenge, I assure you. But you have chosen to make enemies with Sutton, and I have chosen to befriend him. From here, I will head to Northwestern and have drinks with his best friend and his ward. That is how I will execute our plan."

Bradley cackled at the notion. He had to admire the boy's pluck.

"Well, well, you have been busy? Wedding your way into Tom Sutton's little harem, your dog. I suppose he got sick of his ward and has moved on to that sexy little Portuguese vixen. Have you got into his daughter's drawers yet? I'm sure it won't be too hard with that little whore."

John's fist curled under the desk, and he dug his nails into his palms to force inaction. He couldn't retaliate. Bradley had to believe he was on his side, or this wouldn't work.

"You sound like a desperate teenager who wants to impress his school friends." He responded through gritted teeth trying to sound chummy and dismissive.

Bradley laughed, not registering the disgust in John's voice.

"Just be sure to give me a turn when you're finished with her."

John could no longer restrain himself. He had what he wanted, and he had to get out of there before his temper got the best of him.

"I'll be in touch," he said as he rose and slid his glass back across the desk.

"Oh, there is one more thing."

"And what is that?"

"Max."

"Max?" John asked, perplexed.

"If you got all your information directly from Sutton, then we still have a loose end."

"What do you mean?"

"Max also knows about the coins."

John felt weak at the knees. Had Bradley suspected that Max had talked to him? His palms were beginning to sweat, and his heart raced. He took a deep breath and said as casually as he could.

"So, what do you want me to do about it, Bradley?"

"You're going to get rid of Max for me."

"Can't you just fire him?" John's collar was beginning to feel tight around his neck as he swallowed the lump in his throat.

Bradley calmly opened his desk drawer and retrieved a revolver, and slid it across the desk to John.

"But let's cut this cat and mouse game, shall we, it's becoming a bore. Get rid of Max permanently. Understand?"

John hid his fear with a look of the resolution and grabbed the gun, sliding it into the waistband of his trousers and covering it with his sports coat.

"Fine." was all John could muster as his mind tried to conjure some intricate way out of this mess.

"Send Hansie back in." barked Bradley as John pulled open his office door.

Max and Hansie sat on the outside steps, engrossed in a game of whiskey poker.

"Hey, goon, your presence is wanted."

"Don't let your head get too big, or you might get it chopped off, pally." sneered Hansie.

Once Hansie had ascended the steps, John met Max's eyes for a moment and quickly looked away.

"Quick game?"

"Not tonight, Max. I am in a hurry."

"Suit yourself. See you soon, John."

"Yes, see you soon, Max."

Fear gripped John as he rolled his hand over the gun wedged in his belt. Despite being the son of a military man, arguably two military men, John had never fired a gun.

Given John's traumatic childhood, the major had chosen to keep John away from anything that might reignite the violence he experienced at such a young age. All his friends' sons were enrolled in the best military schools in England and Scotland and, from there, were funneled into military careers. But not John. He had never wanted that for him.

Instead, he chose a liberal arts college preparatory school instead, that would foster his son's interests in history, geography, and music. At this moment, John couldn't decide if his lack of experience was a help or a hindrance.

As he approached the Northwestern, he took a deep breath and ran his fingers through his hair. He had to compartmentalize the Max thing for now. One thing he was sure of, he had neither the heart nor the stomach to do any harm to Max.

Weasel and Heidi met John on the hotel verandah with smiles. Cocktails morphed into dinner, which John graciously offered to pay for, seeing he had practically invited himself, and before long, Weasel was struggling to stifle the yawns perpetuated by Heidi and John's robust discussion on swing music.

Finally, he declared that he would be retiring for the night.

"Heidi, I'll see you for breakfast. Don't stay up too late and get into trouble, or I'll never hear the end of it."

As soon as Weasel was gone, John pulled his chair a little closer.

They locked eyes, and he was instantly pulled into her gaze and disarmed. He had tried to avoid an eye lock all night for this very reason. She was stunning as usual, in an ivory chiffon tea- length dress that moved on her body like a cloud. Her skin was bronze-like milky coffee, and her hair shimmered against the candlelight on their table. He longed to reach across her face and push aside the loose tendril that kept caressing her left eye, just to be able to touch her skin.

As the night progressed, it was becoming more and more difficult to harness these feelings he couldn't control. She was so refreshingly unaffected. All the society girls he had met in London weren't interesting like Heidi. They only cared about presenting themselves as desirable for a would-be suitor, listing all their attributes and accomplishments. Heidi, however, was carefree, passionate, and unabashed. She was comfortable in her skin, like no other girl he had ever met. Their conversation had been lively all night, much of the time rolling right over Weasel, who couldn't keep up with all the modernisms.

"Are you tired?"

"No, and you?" Heidi answered, feeling like there was no one else on the verandah but the two of them, despite the loud laughter and constant chattering from the rowdy group behind them. Was he feeling the same way she was, nervous but excited, eager but terrified of failing to be someone she didn't expect?

He looked dapper in his sports coat and trousers. He had definitely made an effort, and she was sure it wasn't on Weasel's account. The pomade that had reined in his wavy hair earlier in the evening had slowly deteriorated over time, aided by the humidity. Now it wouldn't behave, no matter how often he tried to smooth it down. Heidi just wanted him to leave it be. She liked it that way. He was a great conversationalist, as Maria had suggested. And they hadn't yet stumbled on any dark patches or closets harboring skeletons. He seemed like a perfectly sweet young man who, by the minute, was entangling her heart.

"No. Would you like to take a short drive to the Falls. It's a lovely night. There's a full moon, and the stars should be spectacular."

Heidi knew her uncle would probably not have approved, but she had been sitting here talking with him all night, hadn't she. And Maria liked him, didn't she? She smiled and leaned in on her elbows.

"Can I trust you, John Siddley?"

He knew this was the chance to establish a connection with her, to set the trap. Then why was he feeling like such a fraud. He didn't want to hurt her.

"Of course, Miss Sutton. We won't be gone long. Uncle…I mean Weasel…Mr. Byrne said you have to wake up early tomorrow." He was a blithering idiot. Why was he so tongue- tied suddenly?

"Let's go then. We can't miss a full moon, can we?"

Before either of them could change their minds for a multitude of reasons, they were in his Buick together, heading to Victoria Falls. As the wind tangled their hair, they looked at each other and laughed.

"Reckless abandon," said Heidi "What's that?" asked John

This… is reckless abandon. It's that feeling you get when nothing else matters but the moment you're in, and you feel somehow more alive, more one with the world around you."

All he wanted to do was to lean across the seat and kiss her. He wanted the magic of this moment to live inside him, to connect him to the cosmos that shone all around them. His mind swirled with images of Tom Sutton, Bradley, Max, and the gun that poked into his waist.

"I'll give you a penny."

"Pardon."

"A penny for your thoughts."

"Forgive me, Heidi. My mind was just a million miles away."

"I'm sorry that my company is that boring?" Heidi half-joked.

"Oh no, goodness no. It's just that I have a lot on my mind, that's all."

John pulled the car to a resting spot under a tree, where the view of the Falls was magnificent. He went around to the passenger door to help Heidi out. As she touched his hand, electricity rippled through her body, and she wondered if he had felt it too.

John decided he couldn't be this close to her, not right now. His heart was failing him, and he felt emotionally weak when he looked into her eyes for too long. He decided he would take pause and retrieve a blanket from the trunk for them to sit on and discard the gun that dug into his side. He laid down the blanket and patted out a spot for Heidi. They sat together for a few moments listening to the roar of the water crashing below them and staring at the stars, which were indeed glorious against the pitch-black sky.

"I have an early memory of star gazing, you know." started John.

"Tell me." urged Heidi

"Outside our little cottage in Lough Tay. It was deep in the countryside. Rolling green Irish hills."

"But… I thought you were English?"

"I am…but I was born in Ireland. I was little. It was a long time ago." John said dismissively with a voice that belonged to a stranger. Why was he telling her this? Why was he letting his guard down?

"So… you were there at your cottage star gazing with…." Heidi pushed.

"My mother."

"Where is she now?"

"She is gone. But you know, I believed when I was a little boy that she became one of those stars when she died. And on nights like this, I believed she could see me from the heavens, and for just a moment, we would be connected again."

"So, which one is she," Heidi asked

A tear trickled out of the corner of John's eye, and Heidi feared that perhaps she had pushed him too hard, too quickly.

"I'm sorry, John, I shouldn't have pried."

"You don't have to apologize, Heidi. It happened a long time ago."

"I lost both my parents, too, as a child. I don't know what would have become of me if it weren't for Uncle Tom. But at least you still have your father in Salisbury, and I'm sure he misses your mother too."

"Yes, I have my father," John said with a tight-lipped smile. He had already revealed too much, and he had made himself vulnerable.

An uncomfortable silence wedged between them. Heidi fumbled in her handbag for her cigarette case.

"Care for a cigarette?"

"Ok."

Heidi quickly lit both cigarettes in her mouth at once and then handed one to John. Her perfume clung to the air as she passed it to him. It was flowery and innocent and intoxicating. As he took a drag of the cigarette, he was keenly aware of its faded pink lipstick that had been between her lips. He felt nervous just being next to her and quickly decided to start a new conversation thread to distract himself from the electricity that was beginning to spread across his body.

"Why are you so fascinated with going up the river with Weasel? Would it not be boring for you?"

"The adventure, I suppose…the change of pace. Besides, in exchange for some help in his shop, I know Uncle Weasel will take me bream fishing and, if I'm lucky, maybe even tiger fishing, He's not a fan of the battle, but I quite enjoy it. Now that's a real man's fighting fish." Heidi laughed.

"You are a very different kind of girl, Heidi," John said with a smile, and he meant it in the most genuine way.

"Your Uncle Weasel is quite the character."

"He's just Uncle Weasel to me or Uncle Tim, and I should really say, it sounds funny calling him Weasel in polite company. He's always been like a second father to me. Did you know that he was instrumental in saving me from the orphanage where I lived after my father died? He brought me back to Uncle Tom. I know he can be a little rough around the edges, and he drinks a little too much sometimes. He does also tend to get my uncle into trouble, but it's usually harmless. I also know that he saved him, too, once. When I first met my Uncle Tom, he was in the process of slowly killing himself, but Weasel never abandoned him. Those two share a bond like brothers and a dark past, one that neither of them will talk much about. We were all broken in a way, and I like to think that we all saved each other."

This was a revelation to John, who wasn't quite sure how to absorb it all. It certainly didn't line up with the story he had concocted in his mind about his father or Weasel.

"You know there are times when I feel like diving right off this edge in the swirling water below," John said distantly, staring at the Falls.

"That's a morbid thought, John. But I will tell you that many have done it."

"They have?"

"Yes."

"At least they are finally free of their pain Heidi."

"John, don't say that there are other ways to overcome pain."

"Then kiss me."

"What?"

"Kiss me, Heidi, and save me from myself." He looked so vulnerable in the moonlight like he might cry. She couldn't tell if he was faking it or if he was breaking down right before her eyes, and she didn't care which. His wavy black hair tumbled haphazardly around his face, grazing his watery sea-green eyes. His chest was rising and falling quickly, and the heat between them was palpable.

Like a crash, their lips collided, and nothing else mattered. She wrapped her arms around his neck, and he pulled her into his beating chest. Neither wanted to break the connection, and so they continued, switching their faces from side to side without unlocking their mouths for more than a second, barely breathing.

Together they fell onto the blanket facing each other, locked in each other's arms, their hearts beating furiously. Their embrace encapsulated everything around them; the vastness of the night sky, the treacherous roar of the water below them, and the familiarity of the crickets chirping in the grasses around them. This was reckless abandon.

She ran her fingers through his wild hair as he kissed her neck. Is this what it felt like to want someone? Heidi thought. But she barely knew him. John ran his hand over her breast. This couldn't happen, thought Heidi. Heidi severed their connection and sat up erect. She shuffled her hair back into place as blood rushed to her face.

"I am not one of those girls, John Siddley."

"I know, Heidi. I'm sorry." John couldn't help but hear Bradley's taunts from earlier and began to wonder if he really was a cad. "I'm dreadfully sorry. I don't know what came over me. Please forgive me."

"I clearly let my feelings get the best of me too. I suppose I gave you the wrong message." Heidi said, standing and straightening her dress. "I would like to go back to the hotel now."

"Of course." John also stood and dusted off his trousers and straightened his collar. He let her back into the car, rolled up the blanket, and climbed back into the driver's seat. They didn't speak on the ride back to the hotel. Both of them felt ashamed for different reasons. Both felt as if they had manipulated the other. But one thing was clear, and neither could deny that they were falling in love.

John let Heidi out of the car at the Northwestern and escorted her into the hotel. At the stairs, she turned to him and whispered.

"I did enjoy your company John and thank you for respecting my feelings."

John nodded. "Can I come to visit you sometime at Katimo Mulilo? Maybe, then you could show me how to catch that battling tigerfish?"

"I would like that. If you charm my Uncle Weasel…Tim a little, he might acquiesce. Maybe offer to help with the store." Heidi added with a playful wink.

"Understood. Till tomorrow then."

"Till tomorrow."

John watched her ascend the stairs to her room. This was a mess. He could no longer deny that he had genuine feelings for Tom Sutton's ward. He wasn't sure yet how this was going to affect his plan, but one thing was for certain, he could never hurt Heidi.

CHAPTER 6

THE DILEMMA

John watched the burning sun dip into the horizon as he stared out over the Falls. This had become his sanctuary over the last few months. A place where he could come to clear his mind. But the only thing on his mind today was Heidi. He couldn't expunge her from his head or unravel the knot in his stomach created by his deception.

Right about now, he imagined that she would be sitting by a campfire with Weasel at the river. She would be laughing, her eyes creasing just a little in the corners. Her cheeks would be flushed by the warmth of the flames, and she would be gesturing wildly as she entertained Weasel with some elaborate tale. He could be there with her right now, watching this all unfold across the fire, soaking in every smile, every word, every glance she threw his way.

After he had insisted on picking them both up, he had driven them to the boat early that morning, laying on an extra smattering of charm, as Heidi had suggested. As predicted, Weasel Byrne had extended him an invitation, insisting that he would be a delightful addition to their getaway. Just before the boat was untied, Heidi jumped back on the dock and plastered a firm kiss on each of his cheeks. John was completely taken by surprise but was sure he caught Weasel stifling a grin.

Now his feelings were all in disarray. He wasn't even sure about moving forward with any grand plan to sabotage Tom Sutton, and he had done enough already. But if he hurt him, it would most certainly ruin any chance of any future with Heidi.

He was unreconciled, confused, and nervous. This was not how the plan was supposed to unfold.

John was also not a murderer. But until he could figure out how to extricate himself from this mess, he had to make Bradley believe that it was business as usual. He was sure that Bradley could easily have him dispatched, so it was imperative that he keep himself useful in the meantime. So far, he trusted him, and he needed to keep it that way.

Bradley had not yet divulged his ultimate plan to him to destroy Tom Sutton, and he knew that Bradley would renege on their agreement once he had his prize in hand, so it was imperative that he get to the gold first and turn it over to the authorities before that happened. Surely if Heidi saw Tom's thievery for herself, she would have to forgive him for simply exposing it. But the first thing he had to do was get Max somewhere safe. If this plan worked out, he would keep his hands clean and salvage a future with Heidi, hopefully far away from Tom Sutton.

"What now, Mama?" Max yelled in Greek as John pounded on his bedroom door.

"Oh, pardon me, John, I thought it was Mama." apologized Max as he opened the door. "She had been driving me crazy all evening."

Max was a quirky little man with broad shoulders and an easygoing disposition most of the time. He wasn't malicious or bloodthirsty like Bradley's other cronies. John guessed that if he hadn't crossed paths with Bradley, he might have had a normal life with a wife and a couple of children, doing odd jobs here and there. He was good at fixing things. He could have been a handyman. That would have made his mama happy.

However, his lack of natural intellect, coupled with a willingness to please, had made him easy prey for the likes of someone like Bradley. Even John had used his disposition for his benefit, and he regretted it now.

"Max, can you come to my room? I need to talk to you about something."

"Sounds important. Is everything alright, John?"

"It is but hurries. You could say it's a matter of life and death."

"Well, then, let me put on my pants if it's that serious."

"Be quick. I will be waiting for you."

A few minutes later, Max arrived at John's room and let himself in. As he shut the door behind him, he noticed the gun in John's hand.

"You better put that down, John, it's not a toy!" Max laughed.

"Take a seat, Max?" John said without emotion, and Max slowly took a seat in the chair next to the bed, his face contorted in confusion.

"What is this about, John?"

"I told you it's a matter of life and death. Do you recognize this gun?" asked John, pointing it at Max.

"Yeah. Looks like Bradley's. Hey, put that down. I don't understand." stuttered Max beginning to come around.

"Bradley wants you dead, Max."

"Dead? Nah, you're wrong, John."

"I am not."

"There must be some misunderstanding. I just met with Bradley earlier this evening. And John…aren't we friends?"

"We are friends, Max," said John, releasing a sigh and dropping the gun to his side.

"I wanted you to see that this order came directly from Bradley with his gun, otherwise, why would I have it? Look, I'm not going to do it because we are friends. But you know what kind of danger that puts me in the right…to refuse a direct order?" Max nodded nervously.

Do you trust me?"

"Yes. But why?" answered Max

"I don't understand Bradley most of the time, Max," John said, throwing the gun on the bed. It was important that Max knew nothing more for his own safety.

"He wants you dead, and you know he's going to have to believe that I did it," said John pulling a cigarette from his pocket and lighting it.

"You don't have to worry about me, John. I will be out of your hair by tomorrow, or even tonight, if you want me to."

"You'll have to hide upriver somewhere. You can't be anywhere near here. And you'll have to wait there until I come and get you. Understood?"

"Anything you say, John."

"Once I have the coins from Demberra, I will come for you, and we can leave this hellhole for good."

"You will still count me in the deal?"

"We are partners, Max, remember?"

"But I thought you might...."

Max's speech was interrupted by John's frustration.

"No one can know Max. Understand? Or Hansie will be after both our necks." John was sure that the lure of half the gold would keep Max put and his mouth shut.

"As you say, John, as you say."

"Bring only a few clothes, and only what you absolutely need, things no one will notice are missing. If you disappear tonight, everyone will assume you just vanished or had a nasty accident, and Bradley will believe that I followed through. Understand?"

"Can I say goodbye to Mama."

"No, Max. I'm sorry, but it is most important for her to believe that you disappeared, or else no one else will believe it."

"Ok, give me ten minutes."

"Hurry."

Max was back in under four minutes with a bag of necessities, just as John had requested. To avoid any suspicion, they climbed out of John's bedroom window onto the rusty fire escape and down into the back garden. John had strategically parked his car in the alley behind Mrs. Papadopoulos' house.

The night air was thick and moist. The moon was almost as bright as the night before, which gave neither of them comfort. Max continued to mumble words of regret for leaving without an explanation for his mother. After all, they were all each other had here in the way of family, his father having died years before. She could be a thorn in his side sometimes. She was a doting type. But he loved her, and he only wished he could save her from the agony of thinking him dead. John shushed him, and he promised silently to himself that he would make it all up to her when he returned with the money. They'd go back to Greece for a holiday to see all their relatives, and maybe they would never come back here.

"Come on," said John sounding a bit panicked and looking nervously behind them. They closed the car doors quietly. John started the engine, and they were off.

John passed Hansie on the stairs to Bradley's office the next morning. When John had left Livingstone the previous night, he had fired one shot as they drove past the Falls in case they were being followed. Then he had driven upriver and deposited Max and returned by daybreak. This morning, he entered Bradley's office looking well-rested in a clean fresh shirt and trousers and placed the gun on Bradley's desk. Bradley said nothing for a moment but exhaled a puff of smoke into the air and ran his fingers through his already slick hair.

"So where is our good friend, Max, this morning?" he said smugly, eyeing his revolver on the desk before him.

"Gone," answered John definitively, not wishing to elaborate for fear of betraying himself.

"And the body?"

"Somewhere in the boiling pot of the Falls. Satisfied?"

"Yes…Satisfied."

"About Sutton."

"Yes. What about that bastard?"

"It is imperative that he believes that I no longer work for you. I wish to keep it that way to maintain his trust. Henceforth, my contact with you will now be limited. I will notify you by phone when I have the information." John moved to leave.

"Oh, before you leave, kid, Hansie will continue to be your shadow, so don't even think about double-crossing me. He's been following you since yesterday."

"Since yesterday?" John said nervously

"Yes. He saw you peel out of Livingstone last night with Max, but he couldn't catch up to your lead foot."

"I didn't see him at the Falls," John said, trying to sound calm.

"As soon as he heard the gunshot, he made himself scarce. No need for Hansie to get himself wrapped up in an investigation over Max's disappearance. I'm sure his greasy old mama is panicked like a rat in a cage by now. and soon, this town will be crawling with cops." He laughed and exhaled another puff.

At that moment, John realized that Bradley meant to frame him for murder and that he was on a short leash only until he was no longer necessary. He had to quell this fear that rippled through his body and be smooth about this.

"Ah, that will blow over. I'm not worried. Just tell your goon Hansie to keep his distance. He's got me into trouble before, and I don't need him to sabotage this deal you and I have by getting in the way." John said, attempting to sound cool.

"Fair enough. But watch yourself, Siddley. No one has ever double-crossed William Bradley and has lived to tell."

John could only muster a nod as his eyes briefly grazed the motionless revolver between them. Fear rippled through him, but he kept a semblance of calm.

"I'll be in touch then."

"See you later, partner," smirked Bradley extinguishing his cigarette in the ashtray for dramatic effect. John took his leave abruptly, and Bradley watched as he disappeared into the foot traffic beyond his window.

Taking a silk handkerchief from his breast pocket, he gingerly lifted the revolver and carefully placed it back in the desk drawer.

CHAPTER 7

WHEN THE LION KILLS

Maria smiled through the kitchen window as the familiar green Buick pulled off the Great North Road and arrived in a cloud of dust. Appearing out of the dust cloud, John made his way up the hill to meet her.

"Hello, Maria. I cannot tell you how much cooler it is here than in Livingstone."

"Come on out of the sun before you bake. You'll burn that English skin of yours." Maria said, waving to him.

"Where's Mr. Sutton, I mean Tom?" asked John when he reached the verandah.

"Oh, he has gone with Simalala to the south side. We've been having trouble with a lion. It killed several livestock last night and one of Tom's prize bulls."

"I would have been thrilled to have gone with him." Said John genuinely.

"You can still go if you want. I'll have Jonas take you, and he knows the way. The farm truck is parked by the stable. You'll have to drive. Thomas took his horse. Your car won't make it over there. Oh, and when you get back, join us for dinner."

"Yes, thank you, Mrs. Sutton."

"We are back to Mrs. Sutton again?"

"Sorry, I mean Maria," John said, laughing and gripping her hands in thanks before jumping off the edge and bounding down to the stable.

Jonas was only a few steps behind, happily discarding his apron on the kitchen doorknob as he quickened his pace to catch up. After some grunting, the truck engine choked to life, and John turned the car north towards the dam. Jonas beamed a wide white smile out the window like an excited little boy, happy for a bush adventure on this otherwise lackluster Wednesday afternoon.

"Good God, I have told him so many times to fix that thing." sighed Maria holding her ears as the truck grumbled out of sight.

As the dam came into sight, they heard a gunshot. A group of African cattle boys scattered out of the bush and crossed their path to the other side. Up ahead stood Simalala, armed with an assegai in his hand. John hadn't seen Simalala since the cattle incident, and he was both afraid and grateful to see the man again. In Simalala's other hand, he held the reins of Tom's black horse, who was fidgeting anxiously. As soon as they reached Simalala, John cut the engine and evacuated the truck to join the group of men. Simalala walked to meet him.

"Good morning." nodded the impressive African man.

"Good afternoon, it's Simalala, right?" John responded, not realizing that Africans always used a morning greeting, regardless of the time.

"That is right," answered Simalala as he recognized the young man.

"I'm John. We met before…in the bush, with the cattle…."

"Yes, Bwana, I remember," said Simalala without judgment.

"But where is Tom?"

"Behind that thicket over there. He shot the lion."

"Yes, we heard a shot. Did he kill it?"

"Yes, he must have."

"But the horse looks so startled…."

"He can smell the lion, Bwana John."

Just then, Tom appeared from the thicket, a hundred yards or so behind Simalala, his .318 rifle slung over his shoulder. When he saw

John standing next to Simalala, he called out and gestured for them to bring the truck closer.

Simalala handed the reins of the stallion to one of the boys with instructions, and the boy began walking the horse back to the farm as it continued to flail its head. The men climbed into the truck and, after reawaking the growling engine, made their way to where Tom stood in the clearing.

John cut the engine once again and jumped out to greet him. He was oddly glad to see him, and the feeling seemed mutual.

"Good to see you, John. How are you?" said Tom as he gripped the young man's hand in his, and John, wondered for a moment if his father could feel the connection between them. It was the first time they had touched him since he was a boy.

Simalala interrupted the greeting, "Bwana, the lion is dead?"

"As dead as the bull that beast killed. I shot him straight in the heart. He collapsed a hundred yards into that thicket." Tom gloated a little at his accomplishment as he pointed.

"Could I see it, Tom?"

"Of course, yes. We must carry it back anyway…glad you brought the truck. Just follow me, and always keep your eyes on the lookout for the nearest and biggest tree just in case you have to climb it."

As soon as Tom saw John's face turn pale, he laughed heartily and slapped him on the shoulder. Simalala retrieved Tom's rifle, which he had rested against the rear of the truck, and threw it over his shoulder, falling in line behind Tom. Fifty yards into the thicket, Tom suddenly turned frantically to Simalala and demanded his rifle. The lion was gone. But there was no time. A crunching sound came from behind a bush nearby, and the wounded lion emerged.

"Tree!" Tom bellowed at the top of his lungs as the lion charged in their direction.

Simalala was up the nearest tree in one swift motion and had started to ascend. He stopped fast as he saw John rooted to the ground below, staring around in confusion. Quickly, Simalala lowered himself down a little, secured himself against the trunk, and pulled John up like a sack of maize until his legs began to move in assistance. From there, they climbed further up the tree like a couple of baboons, scraping their legs on the rough bark in their haste.

Tom had successfully grabbed the bough of a neighboring tree to their left but hadn't had enough time to scramble any further. The massive animal, with blood flowing profusely from its chest, looked wild. It roared and lurched at Tom's dangling leg. With one powerful lash of its claw, the lion made contact with Tom's ankle, and the man howled in pain. The lion pulled, and Tom tumbled out of the tree, falling in front of the bleeding animal. Simalala and John stared in shock as the lion tore at his flesh. Simalala was not a marksman with a gun, so he handed the rifle to John, making an unfortunate assumption that all white men knew how to use them. The bloody scene below continued to unfold as Tom punched the lion as hard as he could with his wounded chest. There was so much blood it was hard to tell who was more damaged, the lion or Tom Sutton.

Tom continued to writhe in pain as the lion ripped off two fingers on his left hand. He was no match against this majestic beast. Simalala yelled wildly for John to fire a shot, but John remained paralyzed at the surreal sight before him. Time seemed to stop as John watched this man he had hated his whole life literally fighting for his life. Was this what he wanted? Did he want to see him die like this? Did he deserve this? Simalala's screams became more hysterical as he shook the young man in desperation. He had already made a fruitless attempt with his assegai, but the angle wasn't right, and he had missed. Blood now drenched Tom's shirt as he tugged at the lion's tongue, a last-ditch effort to control the beast.

"The ubumbulu[1] Bwana!" Simalala yelled again frantically at John. "Please…please! he is a good man. Don't let him die. Please, please."

Something inside John snapped. Right here and now, the past no longer mattered. This man would die if he didn't do something. The tables had turned, and his father's life was in his hands for this moment. He would be the better man. He would not abandon him

---

[1]　Gun

in his time of need. He quickly lowered himself to a fork in the tree, steadied the rifle, and took aim, avoiding the animal's upper torso for fear of hitting Tom in the process. Whilst praying that his one experience grouse hunting with the major last Christmas would find its muscle memory, he pointed at the lion's rear end and fired. The shot pierced the lion's back. The animal threw its hind legs in mid-air in pain, and Tom let go of its tongue. Another bullet pierced through the lion's torso, and blood and pieces of flesh and fur spewed in all directions. The lion collapsed.

A few feet away from the bloodied beast, Tom lay motionless in his own pool of blood. Simalala and John scrambled down the tree and rushed to his side. As John surveyed his body, vomit came into his mouth. His clothes were shredded, and deep bloody scrapes covered his body. Two of his fingers had been ripped off, and his hand seemed mangled beyond repair. His left ear was dangled by a thin fleshy thread, and his face was covered in blood. He leaned in. Tom's breath was shallow but still viable. Quickly, John removed his shirt and shredded it. He tied one strip along the chewed ear and secured it around his head. With the remaining strips, he bandaged up his hand as best he could.

Then John stepped aside as his loyal friend attempted to save him once again. Simalala lifted the big man like a limp child and carried him to the truck, his back muscles bulging at the weight of him. The cattle boys who now surrounded the truck gawked in horror as Simalala placed Tom in the back. At Simalala's order, John climbed into the back of the truck and cradled Tom's head as Simalala sparked the ignition and lurched the vehicle forward as carefully as he could.

Maria was hysterical at the sight of him and only stopped sobbing long enough to grab some first aid supplies, blankets, whisky, and a fresh shirt for John. They didn't want to move him, so they continued to the hospital in the truck. As John looked down at the man in his lap, who was slipping in and out of consciousness, he wondered if he should have acted sooner. Just one minute sooner could have made all the difference. He could have saved him, for these injuries he was sure were too severe, and death was likely. He could hear Maria whimpering in the front seat, saying prayers under her breath repeatedly. For the first time, he understood how much Tom really meant to her.

He felt helpless as they bumped along the Great North Road. This place was so underdeveloped. In London, Tom would have been whisked away to a modern hospital by ambulance and would be in surgery by now. Chances of survival would have been an attainable possibility. But here they were making this strenuous journey, with their makeshift first aid supplies, including whisky for an antiseptic, to a hospital over seventy miles away while this man's life ebbed away before them.

"Maria, my love Maria" Tom groaned in John's lap.

"Maria… Heidi…my girl, my daughter… I love you, Grace, my darling, I'm coming, Sean, my boy, I'm coming…your Da is coming." Tom mumbled under his breath as his eyes rolled back in his head.

"I'm here, Da. I'm here," whispered John back to him as he stroked his father's brow.

As soon as they arrived at the hospital, they were immediately surrounded by three nurses and two orderlies who quickly moved Tom onto a stretcher and into the operation theatre. Maria kissed his head furiously as John pried her from him and the doors closed.

"Don't lose hope. He is a strong man, Maria."

Hours elapsed in the waiting room. Simalala paced outside the hospital, too restless to sit down. Maria was drained of tears and stared hopelessly down the hallway waiting for any news. John had smoked his last cigarette. The last few hours had been a whirlwind of adrenaline and emotion, and he had now arrived at a state of numbness. There had been no news from the surgeon or anyone for that matter, and the operating room doors hadn't opened since they had arrived.

Somehow in all the chaos, John had had the wherewithal to telephone Weasel and Heidi, but the phone at Weasel's outpost had just rung off the hook. Staring now ahead of him, he imagined how Heidi would feel if she knew. He was, by all accounts, her father. She would be devastated if anything happened to him, and at that moment, John felt the same. Any hatred he had borne the man had dissipated. Tom Sutton was human, flawed like them all. But he was so loved by those he loved. There was so much to Tom's story John was sure he didn't understand, and now he wished more than anything to have the chance to know this man, to understand him, to maybe even love him again.

The operating theatre door swung open, and a tall, thin man with a receding hairline and round spectacles emerged. John and Maria stood anxiously as he approached.

"How is he, doctor?" asked Maria gripping John's hand in fear as the doctor removed his glasses to expose a furrowed brow and consternated look.

"Well, he's alive. If you had brought him here any later, I'm not sure he would have even made it. We managed to stitch his ear back on, but his left hand was severely damaged. A few more minutes and that attack would have been fatal. His body, as you know, is covered in deep scrapes and bruises, and he has lost a lot of blood. He is not out of the woods yet, I'm afraid. If he can make it through the night, though, there is a chance he will survive."

"Oh God…oh God!" cried Maria collapsing back onto her chair.

"Thank you, doctor," said John solemnly, and the two men nodded to each other, and the doctor returned to the operating theatre. He felt just as he had as a child watching his mother die and not being able to do anything about it. This could not happen again. He swore under his breath, hoping God or someone would hear his plea. His focus now had to be Maria. She was bereft, and he was all she had. It was his turn to take care of her.

"I'm sure you want to stay here, so you can be close to Tom. But it's getting late, and we can't sleep here in the hospital. It would do us all good to have something to eat and rest until we know more. Do you agree?" Maria only nodded through empty watery eyes.

"Maybe Simalala should go home to Demberra to manage affairs there, and you and I can stay here in town at the hotel. We can leave the phone number, so the hospital can reach us at a moment's notice."

"Yes, alright," mumbled Maria, glad not to have to think for herself. She pulled a crucifix from under her shirt and rubbed it nervously.

"Do you always wear that crucifix, I never noticed it before?" John asked, hoping to redirect her, even for a moment.

"Yes, it gives me comfort. I noticed that you wear one too."

John pulled his chain out from under the collar of Tom's borrowed shirt to reveal a plain gold cross.

"Yes, it belonged to my mother. And it gives me comfort too."

"Shall we pray together then?"

"I'm not sure God listens to me these days," said John honestly, contemplating all his misdemeanors.

"I'm a sinner too, John Siddley. We all are." Maria said wisely. "But it doesn't stop me from praying."

"Alright then," responded John as he took her hands in his, and they closed their eyes.

"Hail Mary, full of grace…" together, they whispered the prayer in unison, and for a moment, John was transported back to the little church in Lough Tay. He was kneeling on the cold wooden kneeler with one hand clutching his mother's. The morning sun streamed through the stained-glass window above them, reflecting rainbow colors on his mother's face. She turned and smiled at him.

"Thank you," said John releasing Maria's hands as he finished. "I didn't know how much I needed that."

"Is Tom a religious man?"

"I assume he once was. At least his wife was. That's why he doesn't like me wearing this around him. It's too painful for him. I think he buried his faith in her memory. He gave her a cross once, and I suppose that's why he doesn't like to see me wear mine. I never told you this before, but Tom's wife and little son Sean were brutally killed by British soldiers. So you see religion couldn't save her, and in a way, I think he blames God and himself, of course. It's just too painful for him."

John's eyes widened. "He told you this?"

"No, Timothy did. All I knew was that he had lost the two loves of his life, Grace and Sean. He still calls out to them in his sleep sometimes. That's why I fell in love with him, I understood the pain of losing the ones you love. Thomas never gave me details. It was Timothy that explained how they were murdered and how Thomas tried to get back to them, but it was too late. Timothy had had no choice but to get him out of Ireland, so they boarded the first ship out. He had to be forcefully put on a boat that took him to ship. He was out of his mind and had taken to over drinking. It was Heidi that saved him. She reminded him so of the child he had lost. She made him want to live again, and she needed a father."

John's eyes were welled with tears that he couldn't stop from escaping in streams down his cheeks. He had been totally wrong all these years. His father loved him and his mother. He had even tried to come back for him. His heart simultaneously flowed with forgiveness and despair at the thought that he might lose him again.

"That is why Tom will never marry me, John. He thinks of it as a betrayal. No one can take her place in his heart." "But it is my baby, our baby, that I worry about now," Maria said, her hand unconsciously pressed to her stomach.

"Oh my God, Maria, does he know."

"No, and I can't tell him now as he fights to stay alive. You must swear not to say anything…please."

"Alright, I promise I won't. How far along are you?

"Four months."

"And Maria, I must tell you something that you cannot share either. I am his son. I'm Sean Sutton."

CHAPTER 8

SECRETS

By morning, news of the lion's ambush had reached Katimo Mulilo, and Weasel and Heidi were on their way to Livingstone. A telephone call from the hospital early that morning had confirmed that Tom Sutton had come through the night, and he was awake. After a few gulps of coffee, Maria and John made their way to the hospital on foot.

Tom looked like a mummy, bandaged from head to toe. His face was remarkably untouched, save for a deep scratch on his right cheek and the bandaged lump that was his reconstructed left ear. His hand was bundled up like a stump, so it was hard to tell the extent of the injury, and no one dared ask in front of him. His skin was pale and gray, but his attempt at a smile was broad and bright as Maria and John entered his room. He was grateful to be alive.

Weasel and Heidi arrived an hour or two later, and soon the room was filled with laughter and warmth, as they all congregated around Tom's bedside. Weasel had even brought in a flask of whisky and some fat cigars, much to Maria and Heidi's disapproval, which he hid under Tom's coat, which lay crumpled in the armchair next to his bed. John just laughed.

Over the next two weeks, they gathered daily at his bedside as he slowly recovered. The color had begun to return to his face, and his scars were beginning to seal and look less menacing. Even Len, Charlie, and Bert had stopped by several times, as did many of Tom's colleagues and friends in town. Everyone wanted to come a get a look at the man who had survived a lion attack. Tom bemoaned that his hospital room had become like a revolving door of gawkers, and they all knew he yearned to get back to Demberra.

When the foursome wasn't at the hospital, they took their meals at the Northwestern, which had become their home base. The police presence in Livingstone and the surrounding area had ballooned since the disappearance of Max and, with it, a growing suspicion of foul play.

Mrs. Papadopoulos' boarders, including John, had already been to the station to answer questions, admitting truthfully that they had last seen Max alive and well, two weeks prior.

When Weasel insists that John stays with them as his guest at the hotel, John was relieved. He couldn't face Max's mother anymore. A short leave of absence from his job at the bank hadn't been hard, either. Weasel continued to insist that the boy had saved his best friend and that this was the least he could do. Maria and Heidi were also grateful for his company, and he wondered if they had had anything to do with it.

John and Heidi had little time alone during those two weeks, so they settled for stolen glances and goodnight kisses in the hotel hallway near the room Heidi shared with Maria. Their passion for each other had deepened further, bolstered by John's recent heroism, which had only made the young man infallible in Heidi's eyes. Since they were always the last or nearly the last to retire, and most guests were already in for the night, Heidi and John seized that short time to be alone. Maria never curtailed them.

"Don't be too long, Heidi, it's getting late." she would say as she let herself into their room and closed the door behind her. On the second night, they discovered a quiet corner of the hallway under a flickering light at the top of the back stairs to the kitchen.

There, their mouths crashed in the shadows, lingering longer each night, their bodies pressed against each other in a fever that was becoming a losing battle. Their desire for each other was undeniable. They were deeply in love, and it hadn't gone unnoticed by Maria and Weasel, in fact, they seemed to encourage it. But despite his feelings, John felt like he was living a lie.

Since the accident, he had been careful to avoid any confrontation with Bradley. The whole town knew about the lion attack, and entourages of locals had gone to Demberra to see the lion in question. He assumed that Bradley would simply stall his plans for now. Besides, it was unlikely that Bradley would attempt to sneak around there with all the commotion and Simalala on twenty-four-hour surveillance.

He wondered if he should tell Tom about the whole scheme once he was well enough to hear the truth. Maybe then he could get to the bottom of the gold theft once and for all. He just couldn't fathom how Tom and Simalala could share such mutual respect if Tom was stealing from his father. It didn't make sense. Tom was loyal to the core, and John had learned that from the people who loved him most. It wasn't in his nature to hurt those he cared for, at least not intentionally. John understood that now. There was far more to this story than Bradley was letting on, and John suspected that Bradley himself was at the center of it.

And even if he got to the bottom of it, how could he reveal to Tom that he had been by Bradley's side all this time and expect him to forgive him. He had to leave town. That was his only option. He'd notify the authorities of Bradley's intent to harm Demberra anonymously and slip back to Salisbury before he hurt anyone else. The thought of leaving Heidi tortured him most, but he justified that it would be best for her in the end. Someday she would forget all about John Siddley.

After thirteen "torturous" days, as Tom called it, the doctor finally gave the order for his release, under the condition that he rests and not exert himself. As Weasel helped him into the back seat of his shiny new Cadillac, he beamed and handed him a cigar. Maria sidled up next to him and rubbed his arm gently, thrilled to have him back by her side again. John and Heidi piled into the front seat next to Weasel, so Tom could have more room in the back.

Tom looked at Maria with a grin as Heidi rested her head on John's shoulder.

"You two look cozy up there," said Tom suggestively. They both straightened up quickly, and Heidi turned to face him, blushing. He threw her a wink. He liked the boy. He owed him his life. What else could make the young man more worthy? And he already felt like part of the family, like his son in a way.

"Let's go, Weasel! Impress me with the speed of this fancy car of yours and take me home." laughed Tom, and they all concurred.

That night Tom retired right after dinner with some pain pills, and Weasel took himself to bed shortly thereafter. Maria wasn't feeling well for obvious reasons, but as promised, John kept his lips sealed and only bid her a good night's rest.

"I'll be leaving first thing in the morning Maria."

"Oh, but you must stay a few more days, John." She pleaded, giving Heidi a look of encouragement.

"I must get back to the bank, or I'll lose my job." he lied.

"Very well, but you are an honorary member of this family now, and I expect that you won't be a stranger at Demberra. Besides, Heidi is here, and I'm sure you will want to talk to Tom when he's feeling better," she said with a strange look in her eyes that made Heidi feel like she was hiding something.

"Be good, you two." she winked and left the dining room.

John and Heidi were alone at the dining room table. They had both yearned for this kind of privacy, and here it was. They stared silently at each other. Both had thoughts racing through their heads that they dared not divulge. He was more lovely than the first time she had met him, she acknowledged. She had no control when she allowed herself to get lost in his eyes, eyes that seemed so troubled these days. He was hiding something, and it was hurting him, but what was it…did it have something to do with her? He hadn't bothered to style his hair that morning in a rush to leave Livingstone, and now all she wanted to do was bury her hands in it and pull her to him. She didn't want to just kiss him, and she wanted all of him.

Her cheeks were flushed, and her eyes were deep with longing. He was fighting every muscle in his body not to lift her from her seat and carry her away, away to a place where they could lie naked in each other's arms, away from all this treachery and this bed of lies he had created. She deserved someone better than him, this angel girl that had saved his father out of pure love and not a necessity. She was too good for him.

"I have an early morning. I think I will head to bed as well."

"John, don't you want to…."

"You should get some sleep too. Goodnight, Heidi." He stood, waiting for her to rise. It was like someone had punched the air from her lungs. What had she done wrong? She wiped an angry tear from her cheek and escaped to her room before she made a fool of herself. He stared at the empty doorway; his heart felt like it was bleeding.

"You're up early," Tom said as John arrived on the verandah at sunrise, hoping to escape before anyone was awake.

"I am leaving. I must get back. Thank you for your hospitality, Tom." he said, avoiding eye contact.

"Please, if there is anyone who should be doing any thanking, it's me."

"No, please, you don't have to. I did nothing, Tom."

"When I was pinned to the ground by that lion, I came to grips with death, you know. It was only your face, something in your face, that took me out of my body and away from the pain just for a moment. There was something so familiar. Maybe when you're near death, the ghosts of your past find a way to reach you. I should have died and if it wasn't for you, lad, it would have been all over for me." Tom patted John's shoulder with his good hand.

"If you ever need someone, you can always come to me. I owe you my life, and you're like my son. And I will always be there for you."

What he wanted to say was. "I am your son, your Sean, don't you recognize me?" but all he could muster was a feeble "Thank you." as he turned his head aside to wipe the tears that now welled in his eyes. He felt so ashamed. He was a fraud. How could he tell any of them now that he was the one who had burnt the grasslands that fed Tom's livestock and he who had mixed arsenic into the dip that killed his cattle. And it was he who had been secretly plotting with Bradley to destroy him while using his family to do it. It was unforgivable. Instead, he pulled his coat tight and said, "I really do have to go. Best of luck with your recovery."

"You are still planning on going to Katimo Mulilo with Heidi next week?"

"I am not sure. My father is not well, and I may need to return home for a while." he lied, trying to give himself an out.

"Did you tell Heidi this?"

"Could you please? I didn't have the heart to disappoint her." And with that, he slung his bag over his shoulder and stepped off the verandah. He did not look back to see the confusion on Tom's face. It was too much to bear.

He peeled out of Demberra before he could change his mind. A few miles away, he lurched the Buick to a halt under a thorn tree. He could barely breathe; his heart was pounding out of his chest. He took a few slow deep breaths and played it out in his mind again. He would go straight to Bradley and call the whole thing off. After he tipped off the authorities, Bradley would never find out where the gold was buried, and he would be forced to leave Sutton and his family alone. Then would return to Salisbury, to the Major, and put all this behind him. Better that they remember him like this.

He pulled out a cigarette and lit it. He inhaled the sweet tobacco and allowed his heart to slow to a more reasonable rhythm as he exhaled the smoke out the open window. He had been so lost in his thoughts that he hadn't noticed a boy staring at him from behind the tree.

He had been watching John smoke. Enjoying a whole cigarette was a luxury the boy had not yet experienced as he waited patiently under the tree to retrieve the butts John would discard.

"Want one." offered John, holding out a cigarette to the boy. "Bwana, you sick?" said the boy as he approached the car. "No. Why do you say that?"

"You take a long break; I think Bwana is sick?"

This had to be one of Tom's farm hands, he thought. He didn't need this getting back to Tom.

"No, my car heated up, so I am waiting for it to cool down, that's all. But it's all cool now, so I shall be leaving. Here take this and not a word."

"Ah, sure, Bwana!" The boy said, thrilled to have a whole cigarette in hand. "Mina buya na hamba lapa sabenza,"[2] he grinned and disappeared back behind the tree and through the fence from where he had come.

John started the car. He was more determined than ever. He had to be swift because he knew Maria couldn't keep the secret forever, and he wanted to be long gone before that happened. He might have lost his chance at happiness, but he would not see the people he loved to come to any harm.

---

[2] I return and go to work.

CHAPTER 9

A FORK IN THE ROAD

Heidi found Tom on the verandah later that morning, lounging in a wicker chair with his feet propped on the table. This was unusual for him at nine o'clock on a Monday morning. He had peeled back the bandages and was scrutinizing his mutilated left hand. Fortunately, he had retained his thumb and two fingers allowing him to grasp objects like a crab with pincers. He was practicing with the coffee cup in front of him.

"Enjoying ourselves, are we?"

"Don't you dare mock a wounded man, girl!" Tom said with a laugh.

"It will get better, Uncle Tom. I promise." She smiled, pecked him on the cheek, and came to sit next to him.

"John had to leave. Something about his father not being well. He asked me to tell you. He knew how much you were looking forward to this trip. He said he didn't want to upset you."

"You could have fooled me," said Heidi sarcastically.

"What's wrong? I thought you liked him," said Tom with a sly grin.

"Whom?" Heidi asked, raising her eyebrows at Tom.

"John, of course."

"I thought I did, but he was acting so oddly last night. He wouldn't even talk to me. He was so dismissive."

"Maybe he was worried about his father?"

"I don't know. If that was it, why didn't he just tell me? It's something else, I'm sure of it."

"Well, I bet he hasn't left Livingstone yet. Let's stop in and see him before we go to the Zambesi River dock."

"Alright," said Heidi with a worried brow. "Are you sure you're ok to drive tomorrow…with your hand, I mean? I can drive if you like."

"I'm a King Crab now, my dear. I can lock it around the steering wheel," replied Tom as he snapped his claw hand at her. She had to laugh.

Maria was noticeably absent during breakfast again. Her morning sickness had become quite unbearable, but she had feigned another headache and stayed out of sight. She knew she couldn't keep up this ruse much longer. She was beginning to see the changes in her body, and she imagined it wouldn't be long before Tom would come to the realization that she wasn't just getting fat. She planned to tell him tomorrow night at the hotel when they were alone. They had both planned to drive Heidi to catch the boat and then stay over in town.

After breakfast, Tom took the opportunity to light one of his cigars and take a walk down to the stable. It was a bright blue- sky day, not a cloud anywhere. As he sat on a stump by the paddock smoking his cigar, he saw a familiar figure in the distance. It was unusual for Simalala to be out here near the house at this time of the day, usually, he was out by the dipping tanks or touring the fields. Since Tom's accident, they had forgone their early morning meetings, and Simalala had basically taken over the running of Demberra completely. Being out here this morning felt good, though. He felt viable again. He was anxious to get back to work, and he was sure that Simalala would be happy to hear that.

Simalala walked slowly and methodically. His large muscular frame, even from a distance, seemed damaged, but Tom couldn't tell how. Simalala's heart was heavy, and even though he had grappled with this dilemma for two days now, he could no longer keep it from Tom. The sooner he faced Tom, the less agonizing it would be for him and his family.

They had always had more than just a business relationship; it had been a companionship. From their time together in the gold-mines to the rebuilding of Demberra, they had been by each other's sides and had had each other's backs. They had learned from each other's cultures and customs and had shared in each other's joys and suffering. Tom had been there for all five of his daughters' initiations, and Tom and Heidi had cried, by his side, when he had held the lifeless body of his stillborn son four years earlier. Their lives were forever intertwined.

Not many African men in the colonial system had prospered like Simalala. He had taken a chance on Tom the day he had agreed to come to Demberra. He had seen something different in him, and he had trusted him on gut instinct alone. Tom had lived up to his verbal arrangement, and both men's families had thrived.

Simalala now had to make the painful choice to leave his thousand acres and comfortable brick home, which had been the birthplace of five of his children. Early that morning, he had walked the circumference of the kraal that he had helped build. His chest expanded with pride at the sight of all the young families who had found their roots here at Demberra and had built lives for themselves, all because of his efforts. He was so very grateful for this beautiful land that had been so fruitful in its giving. But as he saw Tom come into view, he realized that he would miss the people the most, all the farm workers, and especially Tom and his family.

"My heart hurt, Bwana Tom," confessed Simalala as he reached the stable, his shoulders slouched in an uncharacteristic pose.

"What has caused your heart to hurt, Simalala?" said Tom rising with concern

"My father, he no more, Bwana Tom. He… die."

Tom gasped. Despite Mamba's old age, he had not prepared himself for this news. Simalala's father had always seemed like a mythical creature to Tom, one that would go on forever. Tom had always called him Black Mamba, after the most formidable of snakes, for that reason. Since the first time he had met him, he had always been agile and shrewd, never once showing any signs of ailment or decline.

Tom put his good hand on Simalala's shoulder. Simalala's head remained downturned, his face wet from crying.

"I am truly sorry to hear this, Simalala. No one could ever replace your father. He was a very special man. I am proud to have known him. How did he die? The last time I saw him, he wasn't sick?"

"Matagati,"[3] Simalala said soberly, making Tom nod his head in understanding.

Africans in these parts believed that no man died of natural causes, no matter the age or circumstance. Witchcraft was always at play. Either someone who resented them had willed their death, or they had been killed by a Kalalushi Gun[4]. By Tom's estimation, it was more likely that the old man would have succumbed to malaria or venereal disease if there hadn't been a physical accident.

"Who could have done that, Simalala?"

"I don't know now, Bwana Tom. But I will find my father's enemy."

"Then you will be leaving for your village now? Tom said. "Take as long as you need. I will see that your land is cared for in your absence."

Simalala sighed deeply.

"I go, Bwana Tom. And I do not return. I am headman now and need to care for my people. This is why my heart hurt, Bwana Tom. First, I lose my father, and now I must lose my home and Demberra.

"There will always be a home for you at Demberra Simalala, you know that," said Tom fighting back his own tears.

"Your people need you more now. I will never forget all the adventures I have shared with you, my friend. And we will see each other again. It will give me an excuse to come to Barotseland, and you must come back here too when you can."

Both men stared at each other for a moment, their hearts heavy but full of gratitude. Tom extended his hand to Simalala. This was only the second time in their lives that they had shaken hands, as it

---

3   Witchcraft
4   Mythical gun crafted from human bones that has the ability to fire invisible bullets

was not customary in Simalala's culture. But Simalala took his hand and shook it heartily.

"I go to the house and say goodbye to Dona[5] and the Mtwana[6]," Simalala said, wiping his eyes.

"They would never forgive you if you didn't," Tom said as he threw his arm across the man's shoulders and they Together they ascended the hill together.

------

5   Madam
6   Child

CHAPTER 10

BRADLEY'S SCHEME

BROKE OFF THINGS WITH HEIDI
STOP
COMING HOME TOMORROW
STOP
WILL EXPLAIN THEN
STOP
CONFIRM RECEIVED JOHN

John watched as the post office clerk tapped in his message, and he could feel his chest tighten and the air escapes his lungs. This was not the message he wanted to send, but it was his only way out.

His bag was already packed and waiting at Mama's. He had one last stop, Bradley's, and then he planned to catch the first train out the following day before the Suttons arrived. Once he was in Salisbury, he would send word to Max, and he could come out of hiding. Max's mother's melancholy was unbearable. He so desperately wanted to assure her that her son was alive and well.

He took a deep breath and pulled open the door to Bradley's office. When he couldn't find him at Mama Papadopoulos' house the week before, Bradley had telephoned him at the hotel and suggested they meet. John had relished the idea. This would be the perfect time to end this whole thing before he left town.

He sat opposite the man and clasped his hands in his lap for fear that his nervousness would betray him. Bradley offered him a whisky which John declined but still poured himself one, and leaning back in his chair sipping it, he stared at him coldly over the rim of his glass.

"Our partnership no longer stands." blurted John without apology.

"What do you mean?" Bradley inquired, not sounding as surprised as John had suspected.

"I no longer wish to be your associate. I have failed to locate the gold. So, I suggest you just let this whole thing with Sutton go."

"What, dear boy, why the change of heart?"

"Bradley, I don't know how you're involved with that gold, but I suspect there is more to this story than I've been privy to. Sutton is now lame, and I don't think it's worth your time to pursue this any longer. I have come to find him a reasonable man, and I suggest you make your amends."

Bradley laughed. "Stupid boy. I bet you've been riding that little whore of his, and now you just want me to back off. Your hands are covered in blood, remember that."

John remained still.

"I never killed Max." he spat. "There is no trace of blood on my hands. The gold can never be retrieved, so I suggest you move on. I don't want any part of your deception anymore."

"I stole the gold myself from that old kaffir and buried it at Demberra, you fool. Nothing will stop me from retrieving it once I burn down the place. I heard that Sutton and his family were coming to Livingstone this week…something about a trip to Katimo Mulilo? The timing is perfect, don't you think. I don't think that one kaffir of his will give us any trouble. You see, I just don't need your help anymore. Besides, Hansie is chomping at the bit to see Sutton get what's coming to him after what happened in the bush. Max is of no consequence. He was a dead man the moment he betrayed me.

Don't you see, you have always been just a tool, John, and you will still serve your purpose. Mark my words."

"You're despicable, Bradley. I regret the day I laid eyes on you." John said through clenched teeth. He stood up. He had to get to the police station. He didn't care about how it might implicate him personally anymore. But before that, he had to get to a telephone and warn Tom, Maria, and Heidi before they left for Livingstone tomorrow. He wasn't sure Simalala would be able to thwart Bradley's efforts alone, and Hansie could already be on his way there for all he knew.

As his feet crossed the door jamb, he felt a hand over his mouth. He struggled for a moment, and then his vision spiraled out of control. He was falling. The last thing he saw was Bradley standing over him with a wet handkerchief and a bottle of ether.

It had been a long time since Bradley had undertaken a physical attack himself unless it was on some unsuspecting female, who was far easier to control. A couple of slaps, and they usually shut up and gave him what he wanted. He usually left this kind of gruesome work to his henchmen. He panted as he heaved John's unconscious body to the back of his office, pulling him behind the armchair and throwing a coat over him.

"I still need you alive, John. The police will soon be looking for you," he whispered with a smirk.

He returned to his whisky bottle and poured himself a palpable amount, and gulped it in one swig. Swiveling in his chair to face John, who remained motionless on the floor, he ran his fingers through his hair until each hair was in place, slicked to his blond head. He straightened his tie and looked at his watch. Minutes later, footsteps scrambled up the stairs, and the door swung open.

* * * *

"Did you see him?" Bradley barked as he rotated in his chair to face Hansie.

"I didn't. But this German man Holtz did." Hansie clarified.

"Who the bloody hell is Holtz?" asked Bradley, slamming his fist angrily on the desk.

"Remember the German I told you about a couple of years ago, who used to work for Byrne up the river at Katimo Mulilo. They had a falling out, and that goon Mooi Boetie left him with a dislocated jaw and fractured arm. He's been basically hiding out up there doing side jobs."

"Isn't he the one who prattled to the police about Byrne's secret work?" Hansie nodded.

"Yes, and Mooi Boetie is still working for Byrne?"

"That's right! So, it's this German, Holtz, that spotted him on the banks of the Zambezi, fishing away his time."

"Hmm…interesting." mused Bradley as he picked at the mole on his cheek.

"So where does this Holtz happen to be as of now?"

"Thought you might want to see him immediately, boss. He is waiting outside." Bradley smiled and leaned back in his chair with his arms clasped behind his neck. Hansie stepped out of the office into the small hallway vestibule and returned with Holtz.

Holtz entered and took the seat opposite Bradley. He was of average height and had a paunch belly, accentuated by his trousers which seemed too tight at the waist. He had a large bulbous nose and shifty eyes that looked half closed as if the room was too bright to open them any further. His hair was thin and greying and had been scraped across his head with a comb and greased down.

"So… you have seen Max? My former employee?"

He offered the man a cigarette, taking the time to light it casually for him. The man took a drag and exhaled. When he spoke, it was in broken English with a thick German accent.

"Yeah."

"Where to be precise?"

"Past Mombova. He come wis a young man, bleck hair… Englisch ich denke."

"And you are certain it was the son of Mama Papadopoulos at the boarding house?"

"Yeah. It was Max. I lost viel geld to that griechisch in ze poker, when I came here to Livingstone."

"Honesty isn't one of John Siddley's virtues, now is it, Hansie?" sneered Bradley, and Hansie laughed with his yellow teeth.

"I gather you have no clue what I am talking about," Bradley said, rounding on the German.

"Nein."

"It's of no consequence. Tell me, Holtz, would you like to make £100? I need an independent witness."

"Witness?" Holtz's voice brimmed with confusion and greed.

"Zeuge." interjected Hansie.

"A simple one. I plan to file a lawsuit against a man named John Siddley, the young man you saw with Max. He and Max are default-ers in one of my land deals. They cheated me." Bradley spoke slowly and deliberately. Holtz nodded with comprehension.

"I have sufficient proof against Siddley, but I need proof they were working together. So, I need you to go to the police station and tell them that you saw Max and Siddley together around Mombova on or around the fourteenth of last month."

"Zusammen mit." suggested Hansie.

"Yah, yah, for £100? Verstehe. I understand. I tell police that I see Max and Junger Mann in Mombova." Holtz said, smiling as he extinguished his cigarette in the decorative ashtray that Bradley had pushed across the desk to him.

"John Siddley," Bradley repeated slowly as if the man was stupid.

"Yah yah, John Siddley." The German repeated the name perfectly.

Bradley retrieved his billfold from his breast pocket and pulled out a £50 note, and slid it across the desk.

"£50, an advance payment. You can stay at Hansie's for a few days. I'll pay you the rest after they are arrested." Holtz rose, thrilled with the arrangement, and reached to shake Bradley's hand.

Bradley shook it firmly and didn't let it go. "I warn you, Holtz. Now that you have taken my money, you can't double- cross me, you understand. I know what Mooi Boetie did to you. Hansie will be worse, I promise. I am not Byrne. I don't mess around." He released his hand.

"I am no fool, Herr. Bradley. I would not take money if I cannot do ze verk."

Bradley nodded in appreciation.

"Now go to the police station. Then wait for Hansie at the post office, and he'll give you his address. He may have another job for you." The German nodded and left the office.

As soon as the German had disappeared into the street, Hansie took Hotlz's seat opposite Bradley. Bradley pulled out his billfold again and counted out three £50 notes.

"Hansie. Here. Take this now."

Then Bradley pulled a box from the filing cabinet behind him and placed it in front of Hansie. He lifted the lid, and inside, wrapped in a handkerchief, was his revolver.

"Don't touch it!" Bradley snapped as Hansie moved to retrieve the gun.

"It has Siddley's fingerprints all over it, and fingerprints are traceable. I want it to remain that way…you get my meaning?" Bradley whispered, reflexively turning to the silent heap on the floor behind him.

Bradley removed a set of black leather gloves from the desk drawer and threw them at Hansie.

"Wear these before you remove the cloth and take your target down, then plant the gun in Siddley's room at Mama's place."

Hansie let a smirk escape his mouth and nodded. He shoved the gloves into his jacket pocket and replaced the lid on the gun box.

"If you leave the slightest fingerprint on the gun, Hansie, it shall be your neck instead of Siddley's hanging by the noose."

"As you say, Mr. Bradley."

"As soon as Max's body is discovered by the police, there will be £500 waiting for you to claim."

"Don't worry, and I'll deposit it right under the buttons' noses."

Bradley rose and walked to the heap concealed from view by the large armchair and gestured to Hansie to follow. Bradley revealed his victim.

Hansie laughed at John's limp body. "Impressive boss."

"Go now and find Max and take care of him. After you've done the deed and planted the gun, come back here tonight, and get him when it's dark. He's sedated and won't give you any trouble. Tape him up and keep him at your place. Have the German keep an eye on him; give him a couple of pounds. I already checked with the hotel and Sutton is supposed to arrive here tomorrow, and then the coppers will be crawling all over this place. Then you can lay low until Sunday when Sutton and his crew are en-route to Katimo Mulilo for their little holiday before you torch Demberra. Then we release Siddley to the cops." said Bradley wiping his hands together.

"You might even get a reward boss."

"Wouldn't that be the cake."

"I'll take care of it," said Hansie, and with that, he grabbed the gun box and disappeared out the door and into the stairway. After Hansie was out of sight, Bradley poured himself another whiskey and, turning in his seat, toasted John's lifeless body. The cards were all falling right where he intended.

CHAPTER 11

FRAMED

mama Papadopoulos had no idea of John Siddley's whereabouts.

"He went to the post office to send a telegram yesterday. He was supposed to leave to go home today. See, his suitcase is packed in the hall, but he no come back yet." she had said through red eyes surrounded by dark circles from lack of sleep.

"Her son Max is missing, poor woman," Maria said after they left. "Thomas, you remember him, he was always playing poker on the verandah of the Northwestern. John was friends with him, I think."

Tom nodded, looking a little worried. "After you ladies get what you need at the store, let's get an early supper at the hotel. Weasel will be expecting Heidi on that boat first thing tomorrow, and we can't wait around here for John. He's a big boy. Maria and I will stop by Mama's again tomorrow after we drop you off Heidi to see if he has returned."

Heidi nodded sadly. She didn't want to admit that she had a gut feeling that something wasn't right. The more she thought about it, the more she didn't believe John's reason for leaving. They were close enough that he could have told her if his father wasn't well, weren't they?

Maria, on the other hand, was angry at John for leaving so abruptly and running away from the truth. He had had ample opportunities to tell Tom who he was. She had promised not to betray his trust, but it was getting harder each day. She had been so hopeful that they would track him down here in Livingstone before he left, and he would finally come clean. She didn't understand why this was so hard for him. Didn't he want a reconciliation after all these years? Keeping all these secrets from Tom was wearing on her.

They were halfway through supper when Len Johnston found them later that day in the hotel restaurant. Tom immediately had another chair brought over and insisted he joins them.

"Ugh, Livingstone and its heat," he said, wiping his sweaty brow with his handkerchief and taking the seat.

"Cool off and have a drink."

Len stopped him, gesturing to the waiter. "Sorry, but I will be on duty long into the night."

"Is it something serious?"

"I'm afraid so. The death of a local."

"Who?"

"Max Papadopoulos." Do you know him?"

"We just spoke to his mother earlier today?" Heidi gasped, and she grabbed Maria's hand across the table in shock.

"She just confirmed the identity of the body. She is obviously inconsolable. He was her only son and family here in Africa." Len wiped his handkerchief across his forehead once more.

"Was it an accident?" Maria asked tentatively

"Foul play…gun-shot wound."

Oh, God. Any suspects yet, Len?" Tom inquired.

"I'm afraid so."

"Who?"

"It's against regulation for me to discuss the details, but since you know the man, I must tell you for your own safety. The murder weapon was found in John Siddley's room, and he has been missing since yesterday morning. I know that he has recently spent time in Demberra. If he tries to make contact with you, I request that you call me immediately. He could be dangerous."

"You can't possibly believe that John could have…."

"It seems unthinkable, I know. He seemed like a nice kid. But all the evidence is pointing to him, I'm afraid. It's hard to deny fingerprints and a witness Tom."

"A witness to the murder?" Tom asked incredulously.

"No, not the murder. But it seems that Siddley was the last person Max interacted with, up near Mombova somewhere a couple of weeks ago. Please just be cautious and contact me." Len then stood and placed his cap back on his head, tipping it at the ladies.

As soon as Len was out of earshot, Maria broke the silence.

"No way! There is no way I believe that John could have done such a terrible thing."

"I don't believe it either," Heidi said, her brow wrinkled in worry. "But there was something more to his leaving, I know it!"

"I agree," Tom exclaimed. "You will both leave first thing in the morning,"

"Leave for where?" Heidi asked frantically.

"For home."

"I am staying right here," she said defiantly.

"I shall stay with you, Heidi," Maria said, grasping her hand again.

"Listen to me," Tom whispered, looking over his shoulder. "You are both going to catch the first passenger train home. If John was indeed seen at Mombova with Max, that's likely where he has returned to hide. Weasel knows Mombova like the back of his hand, and so does that henchman of his, Mooi Boetie. Don't like the man but I must admit he has been loyal to Weasel. He will help us look, I'm sure of it. I owe John a debt, and I will find him. The best place for you two is at home. If I'm wrong, his next destination would likely be Demberra, and you can keep him there until I get back. Telephone the hotel with any messages. I will check in as soon as I can. We will get to the bottom of this one way or the other."

"Tom, I think there is something you should know about John." Maria piped up. But it was too late, and Tom had already risen and pushed into his chair.

"We will talk when I get back, Maria. I have to get to the dock." He abruptly left.

Tom assumed that John could be anywhere between Mombova and Katimo Mulilo. Weasel was to meet him at a trading post near the town early the next morning. He missed having Simalala by his side. His hand ached, and having another driver would have been so helpful. He left the engine running, and Weasel and Mooi Boetie came out to meet him.

"I'm sorry I couldn't talk on the telephone. It's John. He's in trouble. Len thinks he killed this Greek named Max. Do you know him?"

"I know him." offered Mooi Boetie without changing his stoic demeanor.

"You do? Have you seen him here? Was John here?" Tom snarled, taking a step toward the large man. Mooi Boetie took a step back.

"I'm sorry…I'm sorry. Look, I owe you an apology from the last time I was here. I didn't trust you. That was my mistake. You've been loyal to my friend Byrne here. I misjudged you. Can we put it behind us?"

A wide yellow-tooth grin spread across Mooi Boetie's face and he offered Tom his hand.

"Better to be friends than enemies with you." And the men shook hands.

Newcomers to these parts never went unnoticed Mooi explained. He hadn't heard anything about John, but he had heard of a Greek who had been staying a fishing camp in Mombova for a couple of weeks. He was apparently a notorious poker player. They left immediately.

CHAPTER 12

THE CINDERS

As the train pulled into Kabi Siding, passengers hurled themselves toward the windows to gawk at the scene unfolding before them as the train screeched to an abrupt stop. Some of the passengers even jumped down from the train to get a closer view. Maria and Heidi froze. Smoke encompassed their dear Demberra home, and angry flames licked at the pagoda as the bougainvillea wilted in defeat. Africans by the dozens had formed a line and were throwing pails of water at the raging inferno.

Maria and Heidi simultaneously became unfrozen and pushed their way through the passengers that clogged the exits. Charlie and Bert had already abandoned the train's engine and were trying to locate the inspector, Joe. They, too, felt pangs of horror seeing the house they had become so fond of over the years succumb to the flames.

Heidi immediately thought of Soleil and Blackie and made a dash stable to find the horses had already been rescued and moved away.

Not being able to locate the conductor, Bert and Charlie crossed the road in pursuit of Heidi and Maria, leaving behind anxious and angry passengers, some of who selfishly wondered why their schedule was even being interrupted.

"Where do you think you two are off to?" The inspector called after them angrily.

"To see if we can help," Charlie called back defiantly.

"I demand that you return to your positions immediately," the inspector yelled.

However, he was unaware of the loyalty these men had toward Tom and Demberra.

"Well, then, I resign with immediate effect. You are more than welcome to tend to all the passengers yourself."

"I second that," said Bert in solidarity.

He continued to blabber on about responsibilities and disciplinary action until Charlie stopped dead on the hill and addressed the passengers directly.

"There are at least a hundred people on board right now, and only two men have stepped up to help these two women. Their house is on fire, and their livelihood is. These are your neighbors. What kind of spineless creatures are you? Will your neighbor be there to help you in your time of need?"

"The man speaks the truth." One passenger exclaimed, stepping down from the train and crossing the road to join them.

"Why are we wasting time then?" Another man said, pulling his son along with him.

"Let's hurry before it's too late." said a woman as she pulled off her gloves and set out to join them.

Before long, over half of the passengers had abandoned the train and were running up the hill to the burning Kimberly brick house. The volunteerism was contagious, and soon more passengers joined the group. No distinctions were drawn between class or gender. Both young and old, women and men, European and African, joined the effort.

"Good speech there, Charlie, you sure know how to get the job done."

"Thanks, Bert."

Rich white businessmen in fancy suits rushed alongside Umfazis with babies fastened on their backs in a stampede to Papa Van Wyk's Demberra home. All these strangers worked in concert. Every possible water vessel had been uncovered from the kitchen, farm, and village. The newcomers joined the Demberra farm workers, who were by now nearing exhaustion. Charlie directed the train passengers to form a line and created a circle from the water tanks, fifty yards away from the house, and back to the water tank. Tin cans, ceramic and clay pots, buckets, and even hats were passed with water, which the front line doused on the burning house.

Some of the braver younger men took buckets into the house and attempted to quell the fire from within. Any salvageable furniture: dressers, beds, pictures, tables, chairs, and clothing, were rescued from every room of the house and thrown out by the vegetable garden to the left of the kitchen.

They proceeded courageously with their efforts until the wooden rafters threatened to collapse, and someone told them to get out. But even when the rafters gave way, the volunteers persisted, determined to vanquish the fire. Maria and Heidi, Charlie, and Bert, black with soot and soaked in water and sweat, were at the helm fighting for its survival. The relentless and continuous soaking eventually gained momentum on the fire. And the fire began to wane under the saturation. Black smoke began to hiss as the flames diminished. As the last few containers of water extinguished the last of it, the crowd that had gathered at Demberra stood silent. They were all covered in black soot, some coughed from smoke inhalation. Others collapsed to the ground in complete exhaustion while younger helpers brought them water and wet strips of cloth to wipe their faces. Remnants of furniture, ceiling boards, and beams lay all around them, damaged and blackened beyond repair. The frame of the Dutchman's house had stood against the odds, thanks to the efforts of these strangers. Despite some smoke damage, parts of the back of the house had even remained intact. Tom's big contribution to Van Wyk's house, the verandah had withstood the flames valiantly but was black with ash and debris. Most of the interior ceilings had collapsed, and the walls inside and out were covered in black soot. The kitchen, where one would likely have expected a fire to start, had been spared.

As soon as it was over, Heidi erupted into tears in Bert's arms. Maria stood in shock as one-by-one, each of the train passengers shook her hand and offered their condolences, as she thanked them graciously for their help. As the last group of passengers made the journey down the hill back to the train, Maria fainted.

Heidi and Bert rushed to her side while Charlie scanned the returning passengers, calling for a doctor. Pushing through the descending crowd, a petite man with a goatee in a black suit, dusty from smoke, came charging back up the hill.

"I'm a doctor. Please…please clear the space. I need someone to get a bed or find somewhere flat for this woman to lie down."

The remaining spectators obliged and continued down to the train.

"You, Miss. I gather you are family. Please come." The doctor said, beckoning Heidi to his side. Charlie and Bert retrieved one of the salvaged guest room beds and brought it to the verandah. Together they gingerly lifted Maria and placed her on it, with the doctor and Heidi in tow. With the doctor now by her side, the two men stepped away to give them some privacy. The doctor firmly pressed his two fingers against her wrist and looked at his watch. He pulled out his stethoscope from the medical bag he had brought along to tend to the smoke victims and listened to her heart, lungs, and then stomach.

"Is she alright, doctor?"

"Thankfully, yes. Both she and the baby are fine.

"Wait…What baby?" said Heidi, slightly shocked.

I'm sorry… you didn't know? Yes, she is pregnant, I suspect about five months along now. She just needs fresh air and lots of rest.

Maria opened her eyes and coughed a little. The doctor raised a cup of water to her mouth, and she drank.

"How do you feel, my dear?"

"Better…thank you. What happened."

"You took in a fair amount of smoke, and together with the shock of it all, you could no longer stand…you fainted."

"Oh!" said Maria, instinctively touching her stomach.

"The baby's heartbeat is strong. I do apologize, but I must leave now and catch the train before it leaves."

"They're not going anywhere without us." chimed in Bert. He and Charlie had heard the exchange with the doctor, and neither was sure what to do given these new circumstances.

"Um…maybe you and Maria should get back on the train and come with us to Lusaka?" suggested Charlie quietly to Heidi.

"I don't think I could stand that journey, Charlie." insisted Maria overhearing him.

"Heidi and I will be fine here. We have our Demberra family here to help us. We will be fine. Could you please telephone Thomas at Northwestern when you get to the next stop and tell him what has happened? I doubt we have a working phone anymore. Please tell him to come home right away."

"Alright…as long as you're sure, Maria," said Bert uneasily. We will stop back here tomorrow if you like."

"Yes, thank you…thank you both for everything."

Please thank all the passengers for me too, will you? said Heidi as she knelt by Maria, holding her hand. "Without them, Demberra would have been completely destroyed." "We are forever grateful."

"We will," promised Charlie, and he leaned down and kissed Maria and Heidi on the foreheads. "Take care of her," he said to Heidi.

"I will," said Heidi, standing. Bert grasped her hands and shook them as if he was endowing her with strength, and she smiled at the gesture.

"Come along then, doc. Let's get back to the train. We will contact Tom as soon as we possibly can." said Charlie grabbing the doctor's elbow gently.

"Get some rest…both of you! And congratulations to you and your husband, madam." said the doctor before he turned and was escorted back down the hill to the train that stood patiently waiting without a word of condemnation.

Maria and Heidi watched the train chug out of Kabi Siding, and soon the smoke from the train had dissipated into the hot evening air, and only its whistle could be heard in the distant. Heidi went down to the workmen and their families and thanked each of them for their bravery and loyalty to the farm. She urged them all to go back to their village and rest. Jonas stood by her side, unharmed and anxious to help.

"Do you think you could make us some sandwiches and bring them out to the verandah? Oh, and a basin with some warm water for us to wash, please, Jonas."

"Yes, Dona," Jonas said and bustled off to the kitchen, entering through the side back door where the fire hadn't reached. Maria had fallen back asleep, so Heidi took the time to survey the overall damage to the house. She thought it best that they remain on the verandah that evening. The house was still too smoky. She searched amongst the discarded items lying around them and retrieved a mosquito net and some blankets. They smelled of smoke but were otherwise unadulterated. She gathered a small table, two chairs, and some pillows and set up a makeshift bedroom for herself and Maria on the verandah. She then went down to the stable and checked on the horses, and gave them water. She came back with Tom's hunting rifle and placed it near the table. Jonas soon returned with a basin of water and some washcloths, followed by a jug of cool water and a tray of sandwiches.

"Thank you, Jonas. You should rest now too."

"I stay here tonight, Dona. In case you need something."

"Thank you!" said Heidi grasping his hands for a moment and getting a little teary-eyed. She knew the little old man couldn't do much to protect them, but the fact that he was willing to try warmed her heart. Heidi took the basin to Maria. She pulled back her tangled, long black hair that was matted to her face with soot and sweat. She wiped her brow and cleaned off her face, neck, and hands.

"Why didn't you tell me that you were pregnant?" she asked gently. "Does my uncle know?"

"No," she said flatly

"This is why you haven't been well…all the headaches?"

"Yes," answered Maria shamefully.

"Why haven't you said anything?"

"I wasn't sure that Thomas would accept this baby or not."

"Why wouldn't he?"

"I am not married, Heidi. Your uncle will never marry me. My baby…his baby will never get the name of his father. I believe that this is how Thomas wants it."

A tear rolled down her cheek, and Heidi caught it with the washcloth and wiped it away.

The sun had almost set on the horizon, but John could still make out the figures on the verandah. He was too late. Bradley, or likely Hansie, had set fire to the place hours ago while he was on his way here.

When he came to Hansie's flat, and his guard had pulled his tape off to offer him water, he had tried to tell him the whole story. Maybe Bradley's scheme was more than he had bargained for. But whatever the reason, when he woke that morning, the German was gone. He managed to escape out Hansie's window, which they had left slightly ajar, by using his elbows. He had got to his car and retrieved the penknife that he kept in the glove box, and painstakingly freed his hands. He always kept a spare key under the back left floor mat because he had misplaced his keys far too many times. At that moment, he had been glad for his forgetfulness.

John made the calculation that heading to Demberra was probably the best thing he could do. Maybe they had all gone home when the town had been overrun by police. Now understanding Bradley's intentions, he feared that Max could be in danger or possible even be dead. He was afraid to go to the police since the German had told him that the police were looking for him and that he would pay for what he did to Mr. Bradley.

He pulled the binoculars to his eyes and allowed them to settle on Demberra. It was a charred skeleton of what it had been. As he surveyed the surrounding property taking in the damage, a lump congealed in his throat. He could have stopped this. Why hadn't he seen Bradley's intentions all along? Where was Max? Please, God, let him be safe somewhere. Why were the women alone on the verandah? Where was Tom? He dialed in his binoculars and focused on Heidi. She was barefoot and was wearing a light blue dress, or what had been a light blue dress that was now torn and covered in black streaks. Her hair hung in chunks around her face. She was wiping her face with a cloth. She stared out in his direction as if she sensed his presence. He kept the binoculars on her. His heart ached. "I love you, Heidi Van Wyk." He said under his breath.

Something wild within him suddenly propelled him to his feet, and soon he was running through the thick grass, covering the ground fast as he raced up the hill. Heidi and Maria saw him approach, and Heidi retrieved the rifle and lifted it in preparation.

"Wait, stop…it's John…it's John!" Maria screamed, coming to the edge of the verandah. Heidi immediately lowered the gun, let it drop to the ground and launched herself off the verandah, and ran down the hill into his arms. They collided, and he lifted her off the ground, and they got lost in a kiss that stopped the world around them for the moment. When they untangled from their embrace, they were embarrassed to see Maria staring at them with a grin from ear to ear.

"I am so sorry, Maria…Heidi. Forgive me. This is not what I wanted. I should have told you. I need…I need your help. I am in trouble. And I have nowhere else to run." John rambled

"John, we know the police are after you. Please tell me that you didn't kill anyone. Heidi said as she unconsciously backed away from the fugitive she had just kissed."

"No killed who? …who?" he asked imploringly.

Max…Max Papadopoulos." said Maria quietly.

Tears welled up in John's eyes, and he flopped onto the steps of the verandah and buried his head in his hands.

"No! No-no-no-no!" he screamed. "I am not a murderer, Heidi," he said, looking up at her, his green eyes swelling with tears. "He was my friend…Oh God, no!"

"I'm so sorry, John. But there must be a logical explanation for all this," said Maria softly as she came to sit on his other side.

"No, no, none of you understands. Look at your home, your beloved Demberra. And Max…"

"When we all first heard it, we knew it was a lie. Didn't we, Maria?" said Heidi as she came to sit next to him.

"She is right, John," confirmed Maria. "That's where Tom is right now, looking for you."

"Oh God!" cried John recognizing that Tom's absence only exacerbated the fire.

"Don't you understand that if they catch me, I will fail to prove it was Bradley who did all of this?"

"Bradley?" Both women exclaimed in unison.

"Max knew about Bradley's secret, and then he told me. That's why he's dead."

"What secret?" said Heidi

"He hid some treasure…gold coins …sovereigns under the old steps of your house Heidi, around the time your father died and Demberra was unoccupied. Then you came back with Tom, and he built the verandah right over it. He has been doing everything to sabotage Tom to get to it. Why do you think he was so desperate to own Demberra? This last attempt was meant to destroy all of it, the house, the farm, the crops, the animals, and even you, if that's what it took. But by the look of things, your farmworkers saved the place. It's a miracle."

"We also had the help of all the train passengers. We aren't sure the fire would have been so contained without their help," confessed Maria.

"You said he stole it? Do you know the gold belonged to?" asked Heidi

"Simalala's father."

"But he's dead!" Heidi gasped.

"Well, I suppose it is Simalala's then…"

"What do we do now?" Maria asked.

"Tom will know what to do. Wait until he returns and then tell him everything I've said. He can then take that information to the police. Tell him to find a German named Hotlz. There was no way I could have killed Max. I have been sedated and tied up for the last two days. He can verify my whereabouts."

John stood abruptly and grabbed his bag, and slung it back over his shoulder.

"I must go now."

"John. Don't go. You should talk to Tom and tell him the truth."

"Maria, I can't. Please just tell him that I didn't kill anyone and make sure he knows about the gold so he can return it to its rightful owner. Maybe Simalala will give him as a reward to help rebuild the house. That's all I ask."

"That's it then…you're just going to leave," said Heidi getting somewhat angry. "No. We will hide you, and you can tell Uncle Tom yourself."

"I cannot face him, Heidi, not after all of this."

"You cannot blame yourself for this, John? It's not your fault." implored Maria.

"I AM responsible for this. I planned all of this with Bradley, don't you see. It wasn't until I realized how wrong it all was and to what lengths he would go that I tried to stop him. When the grass fires blazed, I was there. It was me who mixed the arsenic that killed the cattle. I did it all on purpose to hurt Tom Sutton."

Angry tears full of regret and shame tumbled down his cheeks as Maria and Heidi stared in shock.

"Why?" Heidi screamed. "Why would you do that to us…to me? I thought you loved me." She began to slap him wildly, and great sobs heaved in her chest. "Why, why…how could you? What did we ever do to you? What did my Uncle Tom ever do to you?

Maria finally pulled her back, and Heidi stared into John's eyes, which were deep with sorrow. He pulled the small gold cross from around his neck and rubbed it gently.

"This belonged to my mother, Grace. My father gave it to her a long time ago. My father…Tom Sutton."

Heidi was stunned. Somehow in was entirely incredulous and made perfect sense all at once.

"It was Maria who helped me understand. I thought my father abandoned my mother and me all those years ago. I had hated him with every fiber of my being since. Maria opened my eyes. She explained to me how he really felt about my mother and about me.

You see, he never knew that I survived. And all this time, I thought he just didn't want me."

"You knew all along," said Heidi dumbfounded to Maria. "And you didn't tell me."

"Don't blame her. I swore her to secrecy. I wanted to be the one to tell him…to tell you when the time was right."

"And what…you were just going to run back home to Salisbury and write us a letter explaining everything?"

"Well…I…"

"Do you care for me at all, John Siddley, or was that just a big lie too." Heidi stormed off the verandah and disappeared down the side path to the stable, crying.

"You love her, John, don't you?" whispered Maria after a few minutes, as John stood staring after Heidi.

"Of course I do. I didn't know what to do, Maria. I thought that if I left, I would protect you all from this mess."

"It's too late for that now. You can't hide out here forever either. You must leave at first light and take Heidi with you. Take your car as far as the dam and hide it there, then go on horseback the rest of the way. If you need to hide, it will be easier with the horses anyway. She knows the way to Simalala's village, and he will hide you there until Tom works this whole thing out."

"But…"

"No buts, John. If you are lucky to get a chance at true love in your lifetime, you must seize the moment."

"But what about Heidi…are you sure she even likes me any-more," he said with a weak laugh.

"She adores you, fool. Have some food. Clean yourself up, and I'll talk to Heidi."

Maria found Heidi in the stable, crying and stroking Soleil's mane.

"I know you love him, Heidi." Heidi didn't answer but just sobbed more loudly.

"I just don't understand. How could he…why didn't he…."

"You can't change the past, Heidi; you can always move forward. You know that. No one can make him feel more remorse than he already does. Remember that he has lived a lie for most of his life, believing that his father didn't love him or want him. Neither you nor I ever felt that sort of rejection."

"I do believe I love him, Maria," admitted Heidi softening

"Then, go after him. If it's true love, it's worth it, even if it means not being his wife." They both smiled at each other and hugged. Heidi reached across and touched Maria's abdomen.

"You know, I always wanted to have a little brother or a little sister. I've waited a long time for this moment. And Uncle Tom is going to be in love with you all over again when you tell him. I promise."

With two shoulder bags packed with enough food and water for three days, as well as blankets and a small tent, they set off early the next morning. They both wore a fresh set of bush clothes and riding boots, John's courtesy of Tom's wardrobe. And against their protestations, she made them take the better rifle. She assured them Tom would be home before dark as soon as he had received word of Demberra. There was no more harm Bradley could inflict on Demberra now, so there was no need to worry about her. They were to stay put in Simalala's village until Tom came to get them.

Maria watched as John's Buick crawled on slowly with Heidi perched on Soleil behind it, pulling Blackie along behind her.

"The bullets are in the food bag," shouted Maria after them

"Thank you, Maria," they shouted back in unison.

"Stay safe. Take care of each other." She said under her breath as she placed a hand on her belly. She thought she felt something, a movement of life within her. She smiled and returned to her burnt shell of a home to wait for Tom.

CHAPTER 13

A CHASE

It was afternoon before the sound of a rumbling car engine pierced through the deathly silence that had encompassed Demberra since noon after Maria had sent the farmworkers home to their huts. They had all been working since sunrise when John and Heidi had left to clear debris and rubble at the house. Maria had kept herself busy organizing the clean-up, mostly to avoid thinking about the journey Heidi and John had embarked on with her consent.

One of the bedrooms in the back of the house had suffered little damage and had become her new bedroom, while she had turned the other guest room into a makeshift lounge and dining room until they could come up with a better solution. Any undamaged or repairable furniture had been returned to the verandah or moved into one of the more functional rooms that still had a roof. She helped Jonas prepare ham and bean soup and some fresh bread if Tom arrived before nightfall. She was grateful for Jonas' company, and he reciprocated. Fussing in the kitchen helped to create a sense of normalcy amongst the mess of it all. She didn't relish the idea of the night alone, with Bradley and his men still out there somewhere, and hoped that Tom had received word by now and was heading back to Demberra.

At least John was safe from pursuit, she thought, and Heidi was with him. She immediately recognized Tom's car from the kitchen window as it came into view on the road below. She breathed a deep sigh of relief. When the car stopped, and the doors opened, she noticed that he was not alone. Weasel was with him and another large man, the sculking body of Mooi Boetie.

"Oh My God!" said Tom putting his hands to his face. "How? I mean, what could have possibly triggered a fire of this magnitude?" Tom said as he stood in front of the house in shock.

"Well, it wasn't a cigar, mate," stated Weasel as the three men made their way to the damaged structure.

"Maybe, something went off in the kitchen," Mooi Boetie offered.

"No, look at the kitchen. It's entirely intact. It just doesn't make any sense. This reeks of foul play."

"You don't think…." Weasel uttered incredulously.

"He's done it before, Weasel. Maybe on a smaller scale, but… that's the only explanation that makes sense. Give me a minute, will you?" Tom said as they walked on ahead.

His footsteps crunched on ashes and debris as he walked under the burnt branches of once vibrant bougainvillea that still clung to the pagoda-like shriveled skeletal fingers. Charlie and Bert had told him about the fire, but he hadn't prepared himself for this level of destruction, and he was trying to keep his emotions in check. The Dutchman's house, for which he had had so much respect, lay black and mangled in broken pieces. Great black streaks ran wildly across the remaining whitewashed walls. A terrible sadness came over him, not for the possessions he had lost, but for the Dutchman's legacy and Heidi's home; this home he had built himself in the days of the Voortrekkers, those Dutch immigrants who pushed into the wilderness to live outside British rule. The whole farm seemed to be engulfed in an eerie silence. Even the crickets had abandoned the grass around the house. But there was movement in the kitchen.

Tom barged into the kitchen and clutched Maria tightly.

"Oh, my God. Are you alright? Charlie told me you were hurt, Maria? I am so sorry. I should have been here."

"I'm fine. I am just tired because of the fire and the smoke." Maria said, crawling into his arms like a child and exhaling a sigh of relief as she allowed him to wrap her up like a blanket.

Tom leaned in and whispered in her ear. "Are you sure you're ok?"

"I am, Thomas. I am fine."

"And Heidi?"

"She is perfectly well. We are both fine," responded Maria nervously. She heard shuffling outside the kitchen door and recognized that they were no longer alone. She would now have to tell Tom about Heidi and John in front of Weasel and Mooi Boetie, and the news of her pregnancy would again have to wait.

Weasel peeked through the door. "May we come in?"

"Yes, of course. Please come in," said Maria opening the kitchen door wide

Weasel and Mooi Boetie entered the now-crammed kitchen as Jonas struggled to find a place to stand out of the way of the newcomers. They exchanged some awkward pleasantries, given the circumstances.

"Follow me." insisted Maria leading them out of the kitchen into their now makeshift dining room in the back bedroom. "Jonas, can you bring the soup and bread when it's ready." Jonas nodded, glad to have them vacate his workspace. They did a quick assessment of the damage in the main living quarters and re-congregated in the new makeshift space, pulling up chairs at the table.

"So where is Heidi? Down with horses? Oh God, how are the horses…did they make it?

"Yes, the horses are just fine. Now, Tom, I don't want you to go crazy when I tell you what I'm about to tell you." She was beginning to feel grateful that she had an audience. It might keep Tom's knee-jerk temper in check.

"Heidi is not here. She is gone."

"What do you mean she gone…gone where? … with whom? Tom said, raising his voice quick with agitation and worry.

"John," Maria answered softly, waiting for the reaction. Tom leaned in angrily. "Please, sit down, Thomas. Let me explain." Maria said, trying to keep a level head.

Maria explained how John had arrived a few hours after the train had left the day before. She told them how he had managed to escape from one of Bradley's men, some German called Holtz, who had apparently been with him at the time of Max's murder. Weasel and Mooi Boetie exchanged looks when they heard Holtz's name mentioned in the scheme. Maria went on to relate the story of the stolen gold coins that Bradley had buried under the verandah years before Tom had arrived at Kabi Siding. She explained how all of Bradley's schemes to date were concocted to scare Tom Sutton off the property, so he could own Demberra and retrieve the gold. His final scheme had been the fire.

"But how does John fit into this puzzle with Bradley. Why should he be his fall guy? I thought he stopped working for him ages ago?"

"No. He was involved with Bradley right up until the arsenic in the dip. He was also involved with the grass fires Thomas. But once he got to know you…and Heidi, he tried to stop Bradley." Maria said, trying to soften the blow.

"And that's why he's trying to frame him for the murder," Weasel said, bringing the full story circle.

"And you let Heidi go with him? After he tried to destroy Demberra…and our lives in the process. My God Maria, what were you thinking?" Maria only bowed her head and didn't respond.

"Why would he do that to me…to all of us. For money? For Bradley? I just don't understand." Tom fumed. "My God, Maria, how could you let her go?" he said, slamming his fist hard on the table, causing Mooi Boetie to flinch a little.

"She loves him, Tom. They love each other. She blurted. So, who am I to stop her? I trusted him, and it was the only way to keep them both safe. A farm can be rebuilt, but love is more fragile. A chance at real happiness may only come to you once in a lifetime. Why does loving a Sutton have to be so painful?"

Weasel's eyes widened. He understood before Tom had untangled what Maria had just admitted, and the realization washed over his face.

"Don't talk to me in riddles!" Tom said, sputtering angrily, not following her logic.

"Thomas, don't be blind. He's your son! He is Sean." She couldn't stop the tears that followed and buried her face in her hands.

Tom pulled his hands through his hair and paced around the table.

"I believe he is Tom. There was always something about him. I caught myself a couple of times thinking of Grace when I looked at the boy, and then I just tried to put it from my mind." admitted Weasel. "You can't deny that he doesn't look like her."

Tom was in denial. His brain was trying hard to decipher the evidence before him while his heart was reeling at the idea that his only son had survived and had been right under his nose all this time. He knelt in front of Maria and took her hands in his. She raised her eyes to meet his.

"He…he thought you abandoned him and his mother." She continued softly. "He blamed you. He wanted revenge, and Bradley was his ticket. But that was until he got to know you, Thomas. Please remember he saved your life. And he loves Heidi, and she loves him. He doesn't expect you to forgive him. He asked me to tell you to please just give him a head start to like you did at LOW TAY?"

"Lough Tay…" whispered Tom as he sunk to the floor.

The silence was soon followed by a wail somewhere deep in the recesses of Tom Sutton's soul as his brain and heart arrived at the same conclusion. "Forgive me, Grace." he cried, and all the emotions he had locked away for all those years came flooding back in a gushing release.

Weasel knelt beside him and placed his hand on his shoulder. In an instant, he was back on the horsehair mattress in Maggie's Place in Dublin, and the tables were turned as he now stood over his friend, bracing him as the pain of his loss washed over him.

After his emotional outburst had subsided, Tom gathered himself, and with a clear and focused resolve, he spoke pragmatically.

"Where did they go, Maria?"

"I told them to go to Simalala's."

"That's good! They took the horses, I hope…John's car would never make it."

"Yes! He left his car by the dam." Maria affirmed.

"Good! You and Mooi Boetie here, take my truck, and go to Simalala's village. Make sure my children are safe. I'll show you where the tracks start."

"Absolutely!" said Weasel with a salute, and Mooi Boetie nodded in agreement.

"Wait until I get my hands on that Holtz. The bastard has it coming to him." Boetie said, pounding his fist into his hand in a sinister way.

"Hold off, we may still need him yet. He's an alibi, remember," said Tom thoughtfully. You won't get too far tonight; the tracks are damn near impossible to see in the dark. But they won't be moving fast on horseback. You should catch up with them by tomorrow. Maria will put some food and supplies together for you." Maria nodded.

"And where are you going?" asked Weasel, already guessing the answer.

"To see Bradley, of course," said Tom nonchalantly, pulling his revolver from his inside pocket and spinning the barrel, and snapping it back into place.

"Please, Tom, don't do anything stupid." Maria implored.

"Don't worry about me." Tom tried to assure her, but she was not convinced.

"I assume Heidi took the rifle?" Maria nodded again.

There's another in the stable, behind the tack box. Maria, I want you to stay put and keep that gun close to you. Anything threatens the house, you shoot. Understand? It's unlikely Bradley would come here until he's sure we are all gone anyway." she nodded.

"Weasel, can you take me to get John's car?"

Tom kissed Maria and whispered. "I love you! We are going to bring them both home. And Bradley will pay for all this."

Maria allowed those words to hold her heart, and she waved to him from the verandah. When Tom Sutton's mind was made up, he was more stubborn than she was, and there was no stopping him. She had to get word to Len Johnston before Tom did something he could never take back.

"Don't worry, Boyo, we will find Heidi and John. I promise you," said Weasel as they made their way to the truck while Mooi Boetie stayed back to help assemble their supplies.

"To think your son came halfway around the world to find you, and he falls in love with your ward. Now that doesn't happen every day, Sutton."

"I know," said Tom. "I feel like somewhere deep inside, I knew all this time. But what kind of future will they have now, even if he's free. I must make Bradley pay for what he's done to us all…to the Dutchman's legacy…to Heidi's future. I can't rebuild this. Even if I sell all the cattle, I won't be able to bring Demberra back to what it was. In a way, he has already won."

"Maria's right, though, be smart about this. We can't lose you now," said Weasel as they arrived at the dam. "And besides, no one needs to sell anything. It wasn't too long ago that you saved me from financial ruin and prison, remember. I haven't forgotten that. You've always been there for me, Sutton. So, let's just say I deposited £5,000 with Izzy for you some time back."

"You sneaky bastard!" Tom grinned, hugging him across the seat. "I will only accept it if you give it to me as a loan."

"Ah, go on…you're like a brother to me…always have been," admitted Weasel, a little weepy.

"Don't make me all weak at the knees again, Weasel. This paddy has had enough emotions for one day, thank you."

Weasel shrugged him off.

"Be smart, Tom," Weasel shouted as Tom climbed into John's Buick and peeled off in the opposite direction, heading South to Livingstone.

As soon as Weasel and Mooi Boetie had said their goodbyes and were out of sight, Maria called for the head cattle boy, a scrappy youth with lean limbs and an eager expression. She handed him a note. There was a storekeeper at the local outpost about eight miles away who had a telegraph. If he hurried, she could get a telegram to Len via the Livingstone post office. She handed the youth the note and gave him several shillings to cover the cost of the message and his speedy legs.

"Please, Samuel, hurry," she said as she pressed the paper into his hand, and he set off in the opposite direction by way of the corral.

DELIVER TO LEN JOHNSTON, POLICE CHIEF
TOM HEADING TO LIVINGSTONE
STOP
BRADLEY'S OFFICE
STOP
INFORMATION ON MAX
STOP
PLEASE INTERCEPT
STOP
MARIA

CHAPTER 14

THE FLIGHT OF HEIDI AND JOHN

By sunset, Heidi and John had successfully crossed the Nanzela and Chitafura rivers and had stopped to refill their water bags and let the horses rest a while. Thankfully the tire tracks were well worn, and the path had been easy to follow so far. Heidi had been to Barotseland a few times with Tom and Simalala as a young girl, and she felt comfortable in the bush, as comfortable as one could be on horseback with one gun between you. Thankfully animals generally avoided the road for fear of humans, and so far, their journey had been more tiring than eventful. They had built an awkward silence between them, speaking only out of necessity. The depth of silence was laden with questions that couldn't be answered on such a journey. But a quest for survival has an uncanny way of snuffing out the petty and bitter emotions between people who love each other, and perhaps the long stretches of silence helped to temper their spirits. They had been careful to not overexert the horses, keeping their gait mostly at a walk for the last thirty miles, but crossing the rivers had taken its toll on the horses and on their spirits.

As the sun began to dip on the horizon and the foliage around them became veiled in blue, they decided it was time to stop and make camp. They were both eager and simultaneously anxious to say what must be said. John gathered some wood and dry brush to make a fire while Heidi sorted through their food rations and supplies, pulling out three blankets, a mosquito net, a canvas tarp, and tent stakes. John was impressed with how adeptly Heidi erected their small abode before he even had a viable fire.

"Impressive," he said, smiling, trying to break the ice that was wedged between them.

"I'm a bush girl at heart, don't you know," she said coyly.

"I know. But there is so much about you that I don't know, Heidi. Could you ever find it in your heart to give me another chance?"

"Well, I am here with you, John."

"I know…thank you. I don't think I've really expressed my gratitude properly. I'm indebted to you…both you and Maria."

"Tell me about your mother," Heidi said, catching him off guard. She settled in cross-legged in front of the tent on the edge of their pile of blankets as John continued to stoke the small flame he had mustered. She knew she was treading on dangerous ground, but she needed to understand what had gotten him to this place, and she was willing to wait for the answer.

"You want to understand why I hated Tom so much? John said after a minute or two of silence. Why would I do such things to him…to all of you?"

"Yes," responded Heidi carefully

"I owe you that…at the very least," he admitted. He pulled off his jacket, made a cushion of it, and sat down opposite Heidi. "My father was a revolutionist, fighting for Irish freedom in the day against the Brits. So was Uncle Weasel. Heidi nodded, this much she already knew.

"I knew this even as a little boy, although my parents tried to keep it from me. I wanted to be just like him; he was my hero." John's voice graveled up a little.

"My father was a wanted man, and my mother was scared. I even heard her talking to the parish priest one time after one of the towns near us was burned by Black and Tans…criminals… hired hands working for the British who broke every code of conduct in the book." he clarified.

"Horrible…go on." Heidi urged, her deep blue eyes engaged and full of understanding.

"Well, we were supposed to leave for America this one day when I was about seven. We had our trunk all packed. We were staying in this safe house we had in Dublin…Palmerstown, to be exact, waiting for my father and Weasel to return. I remember that Weasel even stopped by for breakfast that morning. He had lost his brother the night before and he was scared… I could tell. He told my mother that he would be going with us to America because we were all family now. Then he left to get his things and told her that my father would be back soon to fetch us." John pinched his eyes shut with his finger and thumb and squeezed to trap the tears that had begun to well in his throat and sting his nose.

"It's alright. Please go on." Heidi said as she reached for his hand and held it in hers.

"He never came. Instead, these two men pushed their way into our house…Black and Tans…they were drunk. They hit my mother when she tried to defy them, and then they broke everything while we hid in the locked bedroom."

"*Sleep, my child, for the red bee hums. The silent twilight falls, and Eivell from the gray rock comes. To wrap the world in thralls. And lyin' there, oh, my child, my joy. My love and heart's desire.*" John spoke his mother's song in a whisper as his eyes became distant and glassy. These were the last words his mother had said to him, and he recited them as if he had been reciting them every day of his life since.

"Through the whole thing, all she was doing was trying to save me." He said, reconnecting with Heidi, tears now rolling freely down his face as he choked on the memory.

Heidi moved closer and put her arms around him, and they stayed like that for several minutes until John pulled himself away and looked deliberately into her eyes. "They raped her, Heidi, but she killed them both; It was a damn stray bullet that took her in the end and gave me this scar." He pulled up his trouser leg to show her. "When I woke up in the hospital, all I wanted was my father. I was waiting for him to take me away from that horror, but he never came.

I felt like he had left us there to die…all because of his righteous cause. My mother paid with her life….”

Heidi opened her mouth to speak, but John silenced her by placing his finger on her lips. “I know now that he didn’t abandon me. He thought we were dead. He had no choice. But it took a journey halfway around the world and a deal with the devil to figure that out.”

“So, what happens now, John?”

“I don’t know. You should never have come with me, Heidi. These are my mistakes…it’s my messed-up life.”

“If the police had caught you now, they would never have believed you, John. Then what? An innocent man gets put away for life. This is better. We will go to Simalala, and he will get us to the border, and we will be gone, into thin air.”

“We, but why? You don’t have anything to run from. You shouldn’t come with me, Heidi?”

“John, I lost both my parents. I cannot bear another loss.”

“What me?”

“Yes, you! You see, I believe that you and Tom can forgive each other and love each other again. My Uncle Tom has carried the burden of your loss, and your mother’s his whole life…you must know that. And I know deep down inside you love him too.”

“Even so, do you believe he could accept me after everything I have done to him?”

“Yes,” said Heidi definitively

“And you…will you forgive me, Heidi.”

“I already have John,” she said, brushing a tear from his cheek

“Marry me then,” John said impulsively, taking his hands in hers.

“What here?” she said, laughing a little.

“You know I love you. So, when we get to civilization, marry me.” He said emphatically, and he pulled the chain with the small cross from his neck and opened her hand. Placing it in her hand, he closed her grip around it. “It was my mother’s. You are just as warm and kind as she was, and damn clever too. She would have wanted you to have this. She would have loved you, Heidi.”

"And I her," said Heidi, glassy-eyed, as she carefully placed the chain around her neck.

Heidi took John by the hands, and they rose together. She buried her head in his chest, and he wrapped his arms around her, pulling her into him. Their quickening hearts beat against each other as he stroked her hair. Heidi pulled away slightly and slowly began to unbutton her shirt, letting it fall gently from her shoulders to the ground. With their eyes locked, she gently gripped John's shirt and began to unbutton it too. He didn't stop her but gently stroked her cheek and tucked the hair that grazed her eye behind her ear. Bare-chested, he cupped her face, lifted it to his, and pressed his lips to hers.

The sense of longing ran deep within them both. Here alone in the middle of nowhere, they were two parts of the same broken puzzle that yearned to connect. As they stood there, he traced a line gently up her back and into her hair as he unfastened her brassiere and let it fall to the ground. He put his hands gently on her breasts and kissed them. She pulled him towards the tent, and they tumbled backward onto the pile of blankets, skin to bare skin, running their hands through each other's hair, on each other's faces and chests, feeling every contour, allowing every electric tingle to shudder through their bodies, as they grappled with pulling off their remaining clothing.

"Make love to me, John," Heidi whispered in his ear as she pushed aside his unruly hair to kiss his neck.

"Are you sure?" he asked, their naked bodies dangerously pressed together.

"I have never been more sure of anything in my life….be gentle."

He softly stroked the hair from her eyes and kissed her deeply on the mouth. Their tongues intertwined, leaving no room for air.

"You are the love of my life Heidi," John said, staring deeply into her eyes as he lay on top of her, their bare chests crushed together, their skin warm and electric.

"And you are mine," she said, pulling him to her.

Their connection proved to be more than either of them could have conjured in their wildest daydreams, and the wait had been worth every minute. As their pulses slowly returned to normal, Heidi rested her head in the crook of John's arm. They lay unabashedly naked side by side, wrapped up together in the blanket, warm from the energized blood that now rushed through their veins. He ran his finger up and down her forearm as she stared out at the fire that was now blazing and crackling a few feet from the tent. A breeze ruffled the horses' manes where they stood tied to a tree nearby. They lay in silence and watched the sky change color, their fingers interlocked. Nothing seemed to matter at that moment but each other and the red and orange streaks that painted the sky above them as the sun began to dip on the horizon.

"It is a beautiful land." John finally said, breaking the silence. "I couldn't imagine being anywhere but here."

With me, I hope?"

"Of course, with you," she said as she lifted herself up on one elbow and kissed him gently.

"We should probably eat something don't you think?" he said, kissing her nose.

Heidi pulled the blanket around her and stood up. She blushed a little as he smiled at her. She exited the tent and rummaged around in the bag she had brought along and retrieved a small bag of oats for the horses. John watched her as she lovingly fed them both by hand. The horses had watered well at the river earlier, so they would wait until morning to find water again. Heidi had said there were places on the journey ahead where they could stop, and they had to conserve the clean water they had left for themselves.

As Heidi pulled together a dinner for them, John threw some more wood on the fire until the flames were thick and jumpy again. With the water bag slung over her right shoulder, and a container of soup, cold fritters, and biltong in her other hand, she tried to navigate her way back to the tent without letting her blanket fall. It was silly, but she still felt a little embarrassed to be so exposed. John welcomed her back into the warmth of his blanket with a grin. They draped the mosquito net around the mouth of the tent and wrapped themselves up together again. And there they sat, and talked, and ate, and kissed until the moon was high in the sky.

Lying here with his body so close to hers, the crickets chirping around then and the fire crackling nearby ignited a visceral memory of the long hunting trips she spent in the bush with her father. She remembered she would lie awake and listen to the fire crackle and the sounds of the bush around her. She had felt so safe then. She had felt like she belonged. That was just how she felt now with John like nothing bad could happen. Like this was no place on earth she was meant to be but here.

"I don't think I have ever been so present in my life. Do you know what I mean? I've always been wallowing in the past or plotting the future. I like this feeling, being here with you, right here in the present where we ought to be." John said as he peeled back the blanket that she had wrapped around herself and took in all her nakedness. She closed her eyes and waited for their lips to meet again. They collided once more, wrapping themselves together as one, moving in tandem, safe from all the world's troubles in their little tent somewhere in the bush.

When Heidi opened one eye at daybreak, the sun had already begun to penetrate the tent's canvas. She was met with two sea- green eyes and a mop of black wavy hair.

"What are you doing?" she laughed.

"Watching you sleep. You look like an angel," he said, reaching down and lifting the cross around her neck and rubbing it.

"Come here, Sean," she said, clasping her hands behind his neck and pulling him to her.

"I haven't been called that in years."

"You don't mind, do you?"

"Not from you." he smiled and leaned down and kissed her. They rolled together in the mess of blankets until Soleil gave a whinny that stopped them short.

"We can't," she said. "Believe me, it's not that I don't want to, but we have to get back on track."

"I was afraid you'd say that. But of course, you're right."

"Uh, you get up first. I am not wearing any clothes."

"Well, neither am I." John laughed

"Then let's both turn our backs to each other and get up at the same time?" said Heidi, suddenly feeling oddly embarrassed in the stark light of day. They both started laughing like two naughty children.

"No looking, Sean!"

"Not even a little?" he teased, turning around slightly to catch a glimpse as she swatted him playfully.

They managed to get their clothes on through fits of laughter and allowed each other one more languishing kiss before it was all business. Dismantle the tent; clean up the supplies; make sure the fire was out; ready the horses. They still had at least another full day's journey ahead, and as the sun climbed higher into the sky, they both knew that time was no longer on their side.

CHAPTER 15

PURSUIT

"Horses," Hansie said breathlessly as he pulled off his hat and flopped into the chair in Bradley's office.

"I told you he would go straight to Sutton's place. It's because of that girl of his, I'm sure of it. And so, they took off from there on horses?

"Early this morning. I watched them leave and then headed back." Hansie admitted as Bradley stroked his mole and leaned back in his chair.

"Well, it's safe to say they're headed to that kaffir's village, the one who works for Sutton. It's at least a two-day trek through the bush from there on horseback. We will need to head them off with the truck. At least Siddley got to see the ruination of Demberra before he left, that must have got under his skin. And no sign of Sutton or that Weasel character?"

"No, sir. I left as soon as Siddley and the girl took off. Sutton's woman was there surrounded by a bunch of kaffirs, so I got out of there before anyone saw me. I thought it best to get back here as soon as I could and give you the news."

"And still no sign of that German?"

"No. Like I said, when I got back from Mombova yesterday, they were both gone."

"Strange. He held up his end of the bargain and gave his statement to the police. Doesn't he want to get paid?"

"Maybe he was afraid of your wrath because Siddley escaped?"

Well, you'll have to track him down, too, Hansie. The police have already been sniffing around here. They asked me this morning if I'd seen Siddley. They want me to come to the station tomorrow morning and give them a statement. I suppose because Max worked for me. I'm not worried. I have people in high places just like before when they were after the gold thieves. But we can't have any loose ends this time."

"So, we leave first thing in the morning? What about the coppers then?" asked Hansie.

"I'll come up with an excuse later, don't worry about them. Meet me at my place early. Siddley and that little whore of Sutton's will have to stop for the night and rest those horses. So, if we leave at first light, we can get to the village first and head them off."

"But they will recognize me," said Hansie with a tinge of fear at the thought of another confrontation with the Barotse.

"The old man is dead. And we aren't going into the village, you fool; we will wait and ambush them before they even get there. Maybe if you're lucky, you might get to have some revenge on some of those black bastards for what they did to your back." Hansie grinned his awful yellow tobacco-stained grin at the thought of retribution.

Within five minutes, the men had vacated, and Bradley's office stood locked and dark.

* * * *

"Stop right there," said Len in a firm voice as Tom barged into the police station with gusto.

"Sit down. Here," said Len pouring Tom a stiff drink and handing it to him. "Sit…please. Maria called me and told me you might blow into town. She's worried for you. You have a good woman there, Tom."

He did not sit, and he ignored his concern and the drink. "Len, you've got the wrong man. You're making a big mistake. It's Bradley… he burned down Demberra. He…" said Tom breathlessly.

"Sit down…please, there's someone I want you to meet." Tom sat reluctantly.

Len called into the adjoining office, and the German appeared in the doorway. Tom rose defensively.

"What the hell are you doing here?" Tom growled at Holtz.

"I see you remember me, Mr. Sutton. I'm Freidrich Holtz."

"I know who you are, you bastard. You worked for Weasel, Timothy Byrne. Mooi Boetie dislocated your jaw."

The man instinctively rubbed his jaw as he remembered.

"Will you sit down, Sutton, and just listen." urged Len angrily, and Tom finally acquiesced, seething through his teeth.

"Mr. Sutton. I know what Bradley does. I guarded ze, boy. He vas bewusstloss." Holtz looked for help from Len.

"He was unconscious, Tom," Len explained.

"Bradley promised me money to tell ze Polizei that I had seen zem togezer…Max and ze boy, John. But I was wis ze boy, bewusstloss, when that man Hansie go to get Max. Boy told me the whole story when he woke up. Then Max's body here the next day… at ze station. Boy, mit me. They ver going to, how you say… frame ze boy for ze murder und me for ze fire at your house Mr. Sutton. So, I let ze boy go, and I come to the Polizei."

"You see, Tom. I'm with you here. I don't believe John is guilty, either. None of it makes sense. Now we just must find him and bring him in, so we can get to the bottom of this." said Len crossing his arms.

"What about Bradley?"

"He's coming in in the morning to make a statement."

"A statement?" said Tom, his eyes bulging from his head in anger. "A fucking statement."

"Now, calm down, Tom. We must be systematic about this. I have Holtz's statement, and I already have a couple of my men heading back from Mombova with evidence on this Hansie.

"I know that Hansie, he's a bastard Len," said Tom rising and meeting Len face to face across the desk.

"Look, I know the shit Bradley tried to pull on you with the land deal a couple of years ago, and you aren't alone, he has a track record, it would seem. But arson and murder are crimes in a whole other league," said Len calmly.

"Heidi is with him," said Tom deflated, sinking back into his chair and taking his first mouthful of the whisky.

"What?" said Len incredulously.

"Yes, she took off with him," he said with a sigh. He trusted Len, but Bradley had powerful friends in this town. Friends that may be able to wield power over Len Johnston. He wasn't sure that John would be safe if he returned, even in police custody.

"You have to trust me," Len said, leaning into him reassuringly. "Anyway, be realistic…you aren't chasing anyone or going anywhere right now anyway, it's getting dark, especially with your hand, for God's sake. Phone Maria from the hotel and put her mind at ease. Come by the station in the morning, and let's see how Bradley responds to the accusations. He has no idea we have a turncoat here."

Tom nodded uncertainly.

"And don't you go and confront him. You hear me, Sutton? Let the authorities handle this, and keep your hands clean. Please trust me on this. As soon as we have Bradley in custody, we will go and get the two youngsters. Alright?"

Tom looked at Holtz, who nodded at him affirmatively. He felt so helpless. He wanted to barge into Bradley's office and ring his entitled, slimy little neck. But Len was right. It wouldn't help their case. John was a fugitive, after all, and Heidi was his accomplice. He had to be patient. A virtue he had never had in spades.

"Before you leave, I want to introduce you to someone else. Maybe this will reassure you further of my intentions with regard to John." He disappeared into the back office for a moment and returned with a tall, distinguished-looking man in an expensive suit. He was handsome with a strong jawline and well-coiffed gray hair, but his eyes were tired, and his brow wrinkled with worry. He walked with a limp. He removed his hat as he approached Tom.

"He looks exactly as I imagined him," he said to Len in a distinctly off-the-boat upper-crust British accent.

"I didn't know you two had met before, Warren."

"I signed a warrant for his arrest a long time ago. But fate never allowed our paths to cross until now."

"A warrant? For Tom?" uttered Len looking confused.

"Wartime, old chap. Let's say we had conflicting opinions."

Tom was dumbfounded. What a time for his past to catch up with him. What the hell did this man want from him now, and what did this have to do with John anyway?

"It would appear, Mr. Sutton, that we have the same interest at heart."

I beg your pardon?" said Tom defensively

"Allow me to introduce myself. Major Warren T. Siddley, ex-British Army, Irish campaign 1918 to 1922. I adopted Sean after your disappearance." the Major said, pulling a birth certificate from his inside coat pocket and handing it to Tom.

Tom slowly unfolded the document and stared at the black print. A storm surged in his eyes that momentarily erased the past decade. "You were there. It was you who ordered the raid on my house…Grace…"

The Major remained calm and gestured a note of forbearance to Len, who, while trying to piece the story together, had moved to contain Tom when he lurched aggressively towards the Major.

"It's alright, Leonard. He has suffered more pain than most men." He put his hand up, and Tom backed off.

"I never ordered a raid on your house Sutton. Your wife…Grace was never meant to be touched…or your son. It was you and only you we were after. But I cannot deny that the men who committed those atrocities weren't ultimately under my command. I will forever bear that shame and expect I will be judged for it when I meet my maker. That is why I took your son. I hoped that you would come for him, but I made a promise to the memory of your wife that if you did not, I would provide for him…give him a home…be his father in your stead."

Tom was bereft of words. He was simultaneously filled with anger and gratitude, hate and appreciation. When he first discovered that his son Sean was alive, he wondered what would have become of him if he had been left to fend for himself as an orphan after the trauma of his mother's death. Before he knew this man, he had been admittedly grateful that Sean had been adopted by someone who had cared for him so well. But now, knowing who that someone was, he had bad taste in his mouth.

"I have been trying to find you for years, Sutton. I know my son…your son has been consumed with finding you and not necessarily out of a desire for reconciliation but out of vengeance. I knew you were here on the continent before we moved to Africa. After a little digging through some of my military connections in Salisbury, I tracked you down myself. I was convinced that John was bound to find you if he hadn't already. When he requested to come to Livingstone and work for this man Bradley, I permitted it in the hopes that your paths might cross and John might finally get to reconcile his feelings. But as a father would, I also did some due diligence on Bradley as well and uncovered quite a bit of impropriety and gold trading on the black market, which I have shared with the good inspector here. I already knew that John had made contact with you at the time of the cattle altercation, and I very nearly didn't permit him to return after his injuries. But it was your wife, Maria, her concern and care that convinced me otherwise. Through her letters, I came to understand what kind of man you are, Sutton, and I began to believe that perhaps reconciliation might be possible if I allowed this to play out. I never expected it to come to this."

"But I…"

You have a right to know your son and you? You owe me nothing, Thomas Sutton."

* * * *

In a daze, Tom had shaken the man's hand; this man who had raised his son for him, this man from a past he had long since locked away. As he pulled off his boots sitting on the hotel bed, he still had so many questions, but they would have to wait. Was it time to finally make peace with his past? If it wasn't for Maria, he might not have ever had the chance to know Sean again. And Sean had saved his life. He owed so much to Maria. She had become his wife in more ways than he had deserved and had asked for nothing in return but his love.

It was time he made it official. He loved her, and he had to let Grace go. She would always live on in their son. It was Sean now who had to be his focus; Sean and Heidi and a future for them free from entanglements. He fell into a restless sleep crowded with dark images that he couldn't recall upon rising but dreams that left him feeling unsettled and anxious.

After a quick mug of strong black coffee at the hotel bar the next morning, he made his way across town. When Tom arrived at the station, Len was nowhere to be found. None of the sergeants could answer any of his questions, and so he paced irritably, smoking a cigar, waiting for him to return.

When the overweight policeman burst through the station door, he was ruddy-faced and breathless.

"What?" asked Tom anxiously. "What's going on!"

"He's gone. That's bloody what."

"Gone…where?"

"To find John, I assume. His place is locked up. His bush truck is missing from his house. No one could tell me of his whereabouts except the lady at the post office, who said she saw him leave early this morning. Hansie was with him."

Tom put on his hat and made for the exit.

"Where the hell are you going."

"Well, I'm not just going to stand around here. That's Heidi and my son out there."

"I'll gather my men and the Major. We'll be half an hour behind you. I assume you're headed to Barotseland."

"Yes…Simalala's village."

"Don't do anything stupid, Sutton," Len called after him, but the door had already swung shut in Tom's wake.

CHAPTER 16

AMBUSHED

Weasel and Mooi Boetie hadn't stopped that night until the tracks had become hard to follow in the dark. In the essence of time, they had just slept in the car. They had been back on the drive since before daybreak now and remarkably had caught up to the hoof tracks, faint but unmistakable.

"I'm glad they stuck to Tom's track," Weasel muttered under his breath while trying to maneuver the truck out of a hole made by elephant's spoor. Mooi Boetie hit his head as the vehicle jerked back onto solid ground. Up ahead, there were two downed trees across the track, and that's where the horses' prints disappeared.

"I hate those big bastards. They cause nothing but destruction wherever they go," grunted Weasel as he got out of the vehicle nervously to survey the obstructed roadway.

"What do we do now?" Mooi Boetie called to Weasel, who had climbed over one of the fallen trees, to see if he could find hoof tracks on the other side of the barricade.

"I can't see them, there is too much debris blocking the tracks for yards up ahead. They must have gone into the bush. If I know Heidi, she is just forging on. They'll likely return to Tom's path up ahead when they can make it out again." Weasel yelled back.

"So now what…leave the truck here?"

"We're gonna have to." Weasel frowned.

Mooi Boetie cut the engine, and the men gathered a few supplies and the .318 Westley Richards rifle in the back seat, courtesy of Maria.

"Let's go," said Weasel. "I can always use you as bait if something out there is going to get me. It will surely be attracted to a bigger piece of flesh." Weasel laughed nervously, clapping the much larger man on the back.

"Agh…Don't worry. They are just as scared of you as you are of them, like I've always said, man." Mooi Boetie assured Weasel, cognizant of his fear of elephants after a near-fatal experience on one of their hunting excursions years ago.

"You keep saying that, lad, but I know the truth."

Mooi Boetie laughed a little and allowed Weasel to push him on ahead. He carried the rifle. About half a mile beyond the barricade, Heidi and John had tucked themselves and the horses deeper into the tall grass when they had heard the distant rumble of a vehicle in pursuit. John had the gun at his shoulder and pivoted it towards every rustle in the grass or snap in the treetops.

They had heard the vehicle idling, and then the engine cut out and assumed that their pursuers were likely now on foot since the path was obstructed. They could faintly hear voices but couldn't yet distinguish them. Then she caught the familiar lilt of a voice that confirmed her suspicions. She gripped John's shoulder and urged him to put down the weapon.

"It's Uncle Tim," she whispered with relief.

"Are you sure. What if it's a trap. What if he brought the police?"

"Never. I know Uncle Tim. If he is here, he's here for us."

Without further consultation, she dismounted and pushed through the tall grass into what was the old road. "Come on, then." she insisted. John stayed behind, his gun again raised defensively.

"Heidi…please…"

"I'll be fine. Stay here then…I'll go."

"Is it not a brilliant day to go hunting, Uncle Tim?" Heidi called out as soon as she could make out his form in the distance.

"Heidi! Thank God!" Weasel exclaimed, passing Mooi Boetie and rushing to her, taking her into an embrace. He scanned her face and gave her a once-over.

"Are you alright? You're not hurt?"

"I'm fine…we are fine!"

"You know it's safe for you to take us to John. I am not on a hunt. This is Mooi Boetie…he's here for the search and rescue too."

"Thank you," said Heidi nodding thankfully to the large man.

"Come on out, John. It's alright," called Heidi towards the seemingly empty bush up ahead.

John sheepishly emerged, riding Tom's stallion and leading Heidi's pony behind him. When Weasel spotted him, his chest lurched a little. He was so obviously the little boy Sean he had once known, the spitting image of his mother. Why had I not realized it before. When John was within a few yards of them, he dismounted, and Weasel bridged the distance to meet him. Weasel extended his hand to the boy.

"It's been a while, Sean Sutton."

John's eyes welled as did Weasel's, and they heartily embraced.

"Forgive me, my boy. You must know that I believed the rumors that you and your mother, Grace, were dead. I saw them take her body from the house. If I had known you were alive, I would never have taken your father away. We would have found a way to get to you…somehow. If only we had known…if only I had known…."

"We can't change the past, uncle. I know now that you were only trying to protect my father and that he believed us both to be dead. We can only look to the future now."

"Ah, it is indeed Sean Sutton. You are so much your darling mother. What a beautiful colleen!"

* * * *

Simalala had received word from his men that two white men had been seen a few miles from his village on the cattle drive path. They were just sitting in a truck in the bush, apparently doing nothing. Simalala was confused. It wasn't unusual for white hunters to venture into their lands, and the missionaries had been trekking here for years. But these men had not set up camp and had not made themselves known. His men hadn't been able to get close enough to identify them, but one of his father's trusted warriors was sure that one of the men had been a part of the cattle thievery two years before. Simalala decided he would go to them himself and see what they wanted. He brought three of his trusted men along.

Despite the language barrier, Simalala was immediately suspicious when he came upon the men sitting in their truck. His warrior had been right. It was Hansie, the same man that he and Tom had rescued after the cattle incident. The man with him must be Bradley. When he saw his cursed black mole on his cheek, the whole story fell into place. This was the man that was stolen from his father all those years ago.

They spun a tale about young John Siddley, who had abducted Heidi against her wish, and how there was a manhunt being led by Tom Sutton himself. They told the Africans that Tom had sent them personally in this direction to look for the young man and rescue his ward, who was headed in this direction.

Simalala intimately knew how Tom felt about Bradley and his partner Hansie too, and was immediately suspicious but feigned ignorance. He didn't know John Siddley well, but the young man had saved Tom's life, and the whole story of Heidi's abduction seemed unlikely. Was this man here to rob them again? Was it revenge or a trick? If Heidi was involved somehow, Simalala was not about to abandon a rescue or leave these men to find her, so he played along with their ruse and agreed to stay with them and help them on their quest to rescue the girl. He kept two of his men with him but, in his native tongue, covertly sent word back to his village with the third man. They were to be on the lookout for John and Heidi and keep them safe at all costs.

By the time the sun had begun to descend into the clouds in the late afternoon, the men had become tired and irritable. They had been waiting here on the cattle drive for hours, expecting to see the fugitives approach, and now rested under the shade of a nearby tree, mumbling to each other in irritable voices. Simalala wasn't surprised. He knew that if Heidi was in danger and was on her way here, she would approach the village by way of Tom's secret path. So, he sat with his men on the back of their truck, biding his time, waiting for word of their arrival from his village, or nightfall, whichever came first.

He was the first to see the grasses move in the distance as the group approached, and his heart sank. He wished that he could warn them. Why had they deviated from the path, and was that Weasel with them? And another white man…yes, the man from the outpost. The man that Tom had punched. John was with them, too, and he seemed to be walking freely with the others. Heidi was next to him and clearly not in danger. As he had suspected, this had been a trap. He didn't know what Bradley was up to, but he had to warn them.

"I go to them." Simalala volunteered, quickly slipping off the back of the truck with his two men in toe.

"What?" asked Hansie. "What is it kaffir?" he called after Simalala as he squinted to see the figures in the distance.

"Let him go. I'd rather have him go and find out who it is. It can't possibly be Siddley out there in the bush."

"But what if it is them?" Hansie inquired, reaching for the binoculars on the back seat.

"Then we will make sure we have no witnesses, my boy, especially those kaffirs."

As soon as Hansie had homed in on the approaching group and identified them, Bradley and Hansie were back in the truck and following Simalala, trekking slowly behind him. They stopped just far enough away to clearly make out the figures of Weasel, Mooi Boetie, Heidi, and John, as Simalala and his men approached them. Hansie took aim out the left window and Bradley out the right, and in one blast, both of Simalala's men fell on either side of him. Bird wings fluttered, and flocks escaped the treetops in response to the sound. The horses who had been in toe behind Heidi and John bolted into the bush to the right of them. Before Simalala could catch his bearings, Bradley had fired again, this time hitting Simalala squarely in the lower back. His knees buckled, and he fell forward with a roar that echoed to the far sides of the clearing.

Bradley and Hansie pressed on into the tall grass as blades whipped against the side of the paneled truck. Weasel had pulled Heidi and John to him, and together he and Mooi Boetie had ushered them into the copse of trees nearby. Weasel now took up the rear with the rifle slung over his shoulder, but despite his speed, Hansie was quicker and pierced the side of his stomach with a .303 slug. Weasel fell backward, and the rifle tumbled off his shoulder and out of reach.

"Uncle Weasel. No!" screamed Heidi as John wrapped his arms tightly around her, so she wouldn't run to him.

"Come and get me, you bastard!" taunted Weasel as he crawled to a nearby tree, dragging himself up against it, trying to divert the attention away from John, Heidi, and Mooi Boetie. He was a hundred feet from where the others were gathered now and completely defenseless. He touched the side of his shirt; it was wet with blood, and the veins in his temple pulsated.

Simalala groaned a few feet away, deep red blood stained the grass where he lay. He couldn't feel his feet. He raised his head to see Weasel as Bradley's truck inched closer. Mooi Boetie, deemed the best marksman in the group, was now in possession of John and Heidi's rifles as the truck bore down on them.

"Shoot, man, and we kill Weasel and the kaffir. You're outnumbered," yelled Hansie leaning from the window of the truck.

"We only want the boy. We have no gripe with the rest of you." sneered Bradley

"Where are you taking him?" Mooi Boetie called.

"The police. Now drop the gun and come out with your hands where I can see them, or we finish them both." Bradley responded.

"They must have a vehicle parked nearby." Bradley continued fishing for information. "Give me John, and Hansie here can take the others to the hospital. Where is it?"

"It's about two miles south that way. Please help them." Heidi blurted, frantic to get them out of here."

"Just let them go, Bradley. They have nothing to do with this. It's me you want." said John breaking away from the trees and moving into the clearing.

"No." cried Heidi as she lost her grip on his hand and ran to him.

"Heidi, no!" moaned Weasel as he tried to stand but couldn't muster the strength.

Heidi's reaction didn't go unnoticed.

"If they have done nothing wrong, then they have no reason to fear, right Hansie?"

"Right," replied Hansie with his rotten yellow grin.

They had no choice but to comply now. As they exited the car, Bradley aimed his gun at Mooi Boetie's head while Hansie moved in with his gun raised, grabbed John and Heidi harshly, and pushed them toward the truck.

"Can I please see my uncle first?" Heidi begged.

"Make it quick," said Bradley nodding to Hansie as he aimed the gun now at Mooi Boetie and John.

Hansie escorted Heidi to the tree, carefully retrieving Weasel's rifle that lay a few feet away from the immobilized man.

"Don't hurt her. She's done nothing." John protested, calling desperately after Hansie. He had seen and heard of what this man was capable of, and he was terrified. Heidi knelt and placed her hand on the wound in Weasel's side. His face was pasty white, and with each wheeze, she could feel the blood trickle a little from his side. She tore a strip from the bottom of her shirt and rolled it into a pad, and then with another strip, she secured it around his waist. She took his opposite hand and placed it over the spot, and told him to keep pressure on it.

"Heidi…I've had worse. I'll be alright. Help is on the way." Weasel tried to remind her. "Be strong, don't fight him, just do what he says."

"That's enough," growled Hansie sharply and pulled her away roughly. Heidi felt helpless and disillusioned as she was pulled away from Weasel and escorted towards Simalala, the two men who had always been her protectors. Hot tears ran down her cheeks like a stream, and her lips trembled. It was because of her that they both lay here bleeding. She knew that they didn't have much time to get medical help. A few feet ahead, Simalala's life was ebbing away into the hot African soil. Blood pooled on his dark glistening back where the bullet had intruded, and he whispered as she approached him. "I fail, I sorry…." Heidi broke free of her captor for a moment and grabbed the hand Simalala extended to her. He choked his breath, hitching in his throat. "I'm so sorry, Simalala. It's not your fault. It's not your fault…we are going to get help…"

Hansie pulled Heidi roughly away from the dying man.

"Come on, you kaffir lover."

John lurched towards Bradley, but Mooi Boetie pulled him back. "Not yet," he whispered.

Hansie brought Heidi to the truck and threw her onto the flatbed as Bradley leaned against the driver's side door. John was thrown in next, but as he landed, he lunged at Bradley and gripped him firmly around the neck. But Hansie was too swift, and in one motion, he was on the back and had cracked him on the head with the butt of his gun. John fell like a rag doll. Heidi screamed and pulled him into her lap, trying to resuscitate him as blood oozed from the gash on his head. Mooi Boetie saw his opportunity and went for the blonde man from behind.

A shot rang out, and Mooi Boetie hit the ground writhing in pain. Heidi screamed again.

"Not a smart idea," stated Bradly coldly as the left arm of Mooi Boetie's shirt turned red with blood, and he clutched his shoulder in pain.

John began to twitch. He opened his eyes to find himself staring up at Heidi, who was now pleading with Bradley.

"Oh, my God. Please, please help them. I beg you. They all need to go to the hospital right now, or they will die. You don't want to be convicted of murder, do you? Just let us go, and we won't say anything to anyone. We'll leave town if you want." she begged.

"Shut up." Bradley sneered and slapped Heidi across the cheek. He threw Hansie some rope and ordered him to tie John and Heidi to wooden slats on the back of the flatbed.

"What about him?" Hansie asked, looking at Mooi Boetie, who was still on the ground clutching his wounded shoulder, and then over to Weasel, who was semi-unconscious against the tree several yards from them.

"Do with them as you will."

"And the kaffir?"

"That's your retribution Hansie. Pull him over to that tree over there and tie him up. That'll be where his people will find their great warrior, hanging from a tree in the bush." Hansie laughed.

"Here, wipe my gun down with whiskey and leave it over there near Weasel when you go. Douse the two of them with some whisky too. The cops will blame them for the kaffir's death. And it will all tie back to Sutton in the end." Hansie nodded in delight.

"You can't…what are saying. Why are you doing this? You said you wanted to take John to the police. What have they ever done to you?" Heidi pleaded. Bradley gave her another hard smack with his fist this time, knocking her down.

"Didn't I tell you to shut up, you little bitch. Learn to speak when you're spoken to."

"Where are we going? You're not just going to leave them here, Bradley? Bradley, just take me to the police, I'll say whatever you want me to say. I'll confess to everything. Even Max…I swear. Please." John begged groggily as Bradley started the ignition.

"No…no… John, my boy. It's a bit too late for that. I think I'll take you both on a little excursion and leave these four men here to their personal business. We can't have any witnesses, now, can we?"

"Where are you taking us." John cried desperately as the truck pulled away from the atrocity, as Heidi wearily looked at him, and a trickle of blood escaped her mouth.

"I think you two will enjoy the lover's leap over Victoria Falls, don't you think? I thought you would appreciate being together in those final moments."

Heidi stared at John with terror in her eyes, a red mark was now visible against her cheek, and she sucked in her lip to stop it from bleeding. John had seen this look before, a long time ago, and he felt just as helpless now as he had then.

"Don't take too long, Hansie," yelled Bradley from the window as the truck crawled out of the clearing.

"You heard what the girl said. His truck is back there about two miles. Leave no witnesses and lose the car somewhere. When you're back in Livingstone, give me a couple of days and then come and see me for your money."

Heidi and John stared at the parting scene, deprived of words or actions. The fate of the men they left behind seemed inevitable. They could only pray now for a speedy death with as little suffering as possible for these brave souls who'd risked their lives to save them.

* * * *

Hansie pulled Mooi Boetie to his feet and ordered him to help him drag the Barotse man to a nearby tree. Once there, Hansie tied a rope around Simalala's neck, who didn't protest. Then of nowhere, Mooi Boetie shrieked and began to tear off his trousers.

"What the hell are you doing?" insisted Hansie pointing his gun at him.

"Serewe ants," screamed Mooi Boetie as he frantically tried to wipe the ants from his legs with his good hand.

"You should be worried about your life, you fool, and not some ants," Hansie said mockingly as he returned to the rope on Simalala's neck.

As he looked down the man's body to his bare feet, he saw them, hundreds, not thousands of them. The colony had found the blood and his wound and were crawling out from under the man. Simalala let out a desperate groan as the ants collectively devoured his flesh in miniscule bites. Hansie backed away in awe of the spectacle as Mooi Boetie attempted to run into the fray once more but was thwarted as more ants clung to his now bare legs and began to bite him in droves.

Mooi Boetie ran in the other direction, wildly slapping at his legs and trying to brush the vermin from his body. Hansie, now at a safe distance on the rise, stood and watched as Simalala screamed in pain. He quite liked the spectacle and folded his arms resolutely.

"Help! For God's sake, do something!" said Mooi from a few yards away.

"I am. I'm watching them." Hansie cackled.

"You morbid bastard!" Mooi Boetie roared and charged at him in full force, ignoring the throbbing pain in his left shoulder and the biting ants on his ankles.

This time Hansie wasn't quick enough to fire, and Mooi Boetie wrestled him to the ground, landing a hard punch to his jaw. But Hansie could still feel the rifle underneath. He managed to wiggle it out from under him and jab it into Mooi Boetie's bloody and wounded shoulder. The man screeched in pain and rolled to the side. Hansie pushed the barrel of the rifle against his chest and held his finger on the trigger. Blood dripped from his nose, and his teeth, too, were covered in blood. He spat.

"Shoot me, you coward…just shoot me!" Mooi Boetie said defiantly, laying prostrate on the ground.

"No, I have some time and something better in mind. Why don't the two of us just sit here and watch that Kaffir over there being feasted on by the ants?"

He pulled an extra length of rope from his jacket pocket and nudged the Dutchman with his gun. Careful to avoid the ants, he pushed him to a nearby tree and quickly turned the end of the rope into a noose. He dropped one end over Mooi Boetie's head and the other over a branch of the tree, leaving very little slack. He tied his hands behind his back.

"Now, we can have can some fun watching the munt die. Right? You bloody Kaffir lover! Oh, and if it gets a little too much for you, then you can always end your misery and just drop."

By this point, Weasel had thankfully slipped into a semi- consciousness state and was not aware of Simalala's blood- curdling screams as millions of red balls devoured his friend. Mooi Boetie turned his head and vomited. Where there had once been flesh at Simalala's wound site, there was now exposed bone. Each time the once indestructible man screamed for help, his mouth became infested by the ants. When Mooi Boetie closed his eyes to the horror, Hansie took the butt of his gun and poked his shoulder, and forced him to watch.

Hansie soon became bored with the spectacle. The Barotse man and Weasel would soon be dead, and he didn't think he even needed Mooi Boetie to take him back to their truck anymore, he was convinced he'd find it alone. As the sun began to set, Mooi Boetie had begun to look paler anyway, and his legs shook beneath him; he'd be more of a liability than an asset. The groans from the African had become weaker and more sporadic. He walked over to where Weasel lay by the tree and kicked his leg. He didn't even flinch. Hansie carefully wiped Bradley's gun of all fingerprints and pressed it into Weasel's hand, then kicked it a few yards away. He was getting good at this crime scene business, he thought, and pulling out a cigarette, he lit it as he surveyed the destruction he'd wrought.

CHAPTER 17

RETRIBUTION

They had traveled in silence for nearly an hour. Heidi and John, who were tied to opposite sides of the truck's flatbed, stared into each other's eyes, making apologies for what the other deemed was their fault. Heidi had tried to wrench her hands-free, but the rough rope had only scraped and burned her wrists in the process. When they had tried to speak to each other earlier, Bradley had threatened them, so they had resorted to telepathy.

Although his wrists burned in pain, too, John had managed to work the rope that bound his hands and been able to loosen it a little. He had tried to convey this to Heidi through head gestures and lip reading. Suddenly, Bradley pulled the truck off the path into an area of bush, where he could maneuver the vehicle around some trees and cut the engine. Neither of the captives knew what he was up to, so when the driver's door squeaked open, and Bradley emerged at the back of the truck lighting a cigarette, both Heidi and John feared the worst.

"We are going to take a little break in our travels. That little visit from the police last night was enough of a tip. I knew Sutton couldn't bear to let the police handle this alone. So, until Sutton passes us, we wait. He'll be tied up for a while crying over his dead friends." smirked Bradley, and he lit a cigarette and inhaled. John saw an opportunity, he and Heidi exchanged glances.

"Can I please relieve myself," asked Heidi deciphering John's thoughts.

"Fine," said Bradley. With his cigarette between his teeth, he released Heidi from the truck handle. Her hands were still bound.

"Bradley, at least undo her hands. You aren't scared of her, are you?" John taunted.

"I am not scared of anyone, Siddley, least of all you. I'll untie her hands. But one wrong move, girl, and I'll blow his brains out." sneered Bradley as he waved his gun at John and took another pull of his cigarette.

"Can I at least offer him some water?" said Heidi as soon as her hands were free from the rope.

"No! You'll soon have all the water you could possibly wish for in a matter of hours, darling." he laughed. "Now go before I change my mind."

Heidi scrambled off the back of the truck, and she looked back at John, trying desperately to interpret what he was concocting.

"Go on. Hurry it up!" said Bradley kicking dirt at Heidi as she walked away from the truck.

Heidi disappeared behind a tree not too far away as a slow smile crept over Bradley's face.

"You know what...I want to thank you for the suggestion Siddley." Bradley sneered as he extinguished his cigarette on the back of the flatbed. "It was only right to untie her. I prefer a little fight from my whores. It's no fun when they're retrained.

"Bradley... don't!" growled John squirming in his restraint.

"Mm, just relax, dear boy, this won't take long, even if she fights back." laughed Bradley as he began to unbutton his belt and approach Heidi's tree. When he was only a few feet away, Heidi reemerged, and instantly she knew it was an ambush. She looked like a frightened buck in a hunter's sight.

"Bradley, don't do this!" screamed John as he continued to struggle to get his hands loose.

"Why not? You've had your fun with her, why can't I?" he said over his shoulder as he ran his hand through his hair and closed the gap between himself and Heidi, who remained frozen.

"Heidi, run!" shouted John.

"I wouldn't do that, Heidi," said Bradley calmly, aiming the gun at John. "He's tied up, remember. You run; he dies."

"Heidi, please…" begged John as Bradley dropped his belt in the tall grass, unzipped his trousers, and reached his groping hand towards her with an expression so vile that Heidi visibly shuddered in fear, as tears welled in her eyes.

"Come on now. Let's make this fun for your lover, boy, shall we? He'll have a nice view from here don't you think?" Bradley snarled as he grabbed her roughly and pushed himself against her into the rough bark of the tree, ignoring the screams of rage emanating from the truck behind him. She could feel his erection against her waist as he ripped her shirt open in one swift motion, buttons flying in every direction. He grabbed her breast, pulling her brassiere down roughly to expose it. He moved in with his mouth biting down hard. She resisted screaming with every fiber of her being. John cried out again and closed his eyes, fearing to witness what would come next. His wrists bled for want of trying to free himself.

"Inyopka!"[7] Heidi suddenly screamed at the top of her lungs, causing Bradley to release her and jump back in fear.

"Where, where?" screamed Bradley waving his gun around nervously while trying to hold his trousers up.

"There, there," she screamed with a convincing shriek as she pointed wildly to the area near a thorn bush a few feet from them. Bradley didn't need further confirmation and ran straight for the truck. Heidi followed suit, keeping up the ruse, but picked up a rock in the process, keeping it hidden behind her back.

"Get back on the truck," he ordered as he quickly closed the cab door. Any stimulation he had felt moments before had completely dissipated. He hated the bush; it was so uncivilized. Bradley mum-

---

[7] Snake

bled to himself as he rustled around in the cab for a flask of liquor to quell his nerves, giving Heidi just enough time to loosen the top knot on John's wrists and drop the rock behind him. Just then, they heard the roar of a car engine approaching. John immediately recognized the rumble of his Buick: it could only be Tom. Bradley quickly opened his door and stepped on the footboard, and pointed the gun at Heidi, thwarting any attempt at escape.

"You try anything, I kill her," he whispered definitively to John. "And you scream, and I put a bullet in his head…understand?" he told Heidi as he swung the gun back at John. They nodded their heads in affirmation but read each other's plotting thoughts. Heidi presumed that John's hands were likely freed by now. They knew they wouldn't stand a chance of escape yet, but at least they could be prepared. They just had to bide their time.

The Buick roared past in a cloud of dust that even reached their hiding spot several yards from the road. A car engine in this remote part of the bush would be a giveaway, so they sat there in silence for at least thirty minutes until Bradley was sure that Tom was out of earshot. Then he lowered the gun and took another swig of whisky from his flask.

"Look at you, you look worse than a Kaffir woman," grunted Bradley as his eyes came to rest on Heidi's open shirt and bloodied brassiere. Heidi quickly tried to close her shirt and avoid eye contact, hoping that her unkempt state might deter him. Bradley retrieved the rope that had bound her hands before.

"I'm not done with you, young lady." he scoffed as he wrenched her hands tightly behind her and tied them to the handle. "I promise you I'll be the last man who has you before I send you over the Falls." Bradley laughed as he pulled her up by the chin and kissed her cruelly on her bloodied lip." "Mm, I am so going to enjoy it!"

As soon as he was back in the cab and the engine once again choked to life, Heidi spat any taste of him from her mouth.

"Heidi…" said John tenderly, not knowing what words would comfort her. "I love you."

"We are not going to die today, Sean. We are not going to die today!" she said defiantly.

As Bradley attempted to turn the vehicle back onto the road, they all heard the distinct sound of police sirens heading their way. For the first time, Bradley was caught off guard. He cut the engine abruptly and rounded on his captives, demanding silence once more as he held the gun at John's head. A mere fifteen minutes later, the roar of the Buick returned and passed them, heading back towards Livingstone. Tom was in search of Bradley. This was alright, theorized Bradley. Hansie would be long gone by now, and any witnesses would be dead. No one knew where he was going. Tom would be likely to go to his office or even his home. Again, he waited until the cars in both directions were far enough away before he started his engine again. He had to get to the Falls and get rid of the evidence. Besides, it would be poetic.

* * * *

Tom gripped the wheel tightly. It was still a few miles to Simalala's village. He prayed to God that he would find John and Heidi there safely, with Weasel and Mooi Boetie, all waiting for him to arrive with the news. Up ahead, Soleil wandered onto the dirt thoroughfare, and Tom slammed on his brakes. Blackie, his stallion, followed behind, emerging from the bush to the left. What were they doing here so far from the village and without their riders? Tom cut the engine and called to the horses, who bounded towards him, happy to hear a familiar voice. "Easy there, where is Heidi?" he said as he petted the horses' muzzles.

He left the car where it was and mounted his horse, pulling Soleil alongside him, and headed into the bush from where the horses had emerged. He was careful to make his way through the denser bush, shielded by a canopy of trees. As he approached the clearing up ahead, he brought the horses to a halt, and through the trees in the clearing beyond, he could see a figure crouching beside a tree. He could barely make it out, but it was a man, and he had fair hair. The man was clearly hiding. He must have heard the car engine, thought Tom.

Tom dismounted and waited for the man to feel comfortable again before he made his move. He could now see that it was Hansie as the bearded man came out into the clearing, moving his rifle from side to side, ready to take out anything that moved. This was an advantage. Tom could see even from this distance that it was his Westley Richard's .318 rifle that Hansie had in his hands.

Tom gave the Palomino a swift slap on the backside. "Sorry, girl," he said to Soleil as she took off back to the road in fright. He held back his stallion. As Tom suspected, the rustle in the bush spooked Hansie, and he fired off two shots, widely missing them. To Hansie's right, a flock of birds took flight in a swarm at the sound of the gun, and he fired two more shots in the other direction. Next, Tom slapped the rear end of his horse, and the stallion trampled his way back out to the road, causing a ruckus back in the trees. Hansie fired again and missed. Tom waited a few moments as Hansie made his way closer to the trees where he was hiding, and then using a long branch, he rustled the tall grass near the edge of the trees, and Hansie fired at the intruder. Six shots, and Tom knew the barrel was empty. Tom charged into the clearing as Hansie raised the gun to take aim.

"Be careful when you steal another man's gun, you bastard!"

Hansie quickly discarded the rifle and made a run for it. Tom aimed his revolver at the moving target.

"You cannot kill me, Sutton," Hansie screamed as the shot missed him by a hair. Tom caught up with him and grabbed him by the back of the shirt. They were now a few yards away from Mooi Boetie, who was still noose tied to a tree up ahead, the shoulder and arm of his shirt stained dark with blood.

"Let him loose right now," Tom bellowed as he poked the revolver into Hansie's back. Hansie scrambled and unknotted the noose from around Mooi Boetie's neck as the man collapsed in sheer exhaustion.

Tom pushed Hansie against the tree with the barrel of his gun and had him put his hands behind his head as he turned his attention to the wounded man. A grueling whimper came from another tree a few yards away. When Tom turned, horror washed the color from his face.

"Help him, Mr. Sutton." Mooi Boetie said desperately.

"Here. Shoot him if he breathes too heavily," said Tom handing Mooi Boetie his revolver.

Mooi Boetie grabbed the revolver from Tom.

"I'm alright…just help him." insisted the traumatized man, who had been listening to the wailing of this dying man for what had seemed like hours.

Despite the mountain of ants that still crawled all over the man's body, Simalala was still breathing. Tom knelt beside him and placed his arm around his neck, and pulled him up. Parts of bone were exposed on his arms and legs, where the ants had devoured his flesh. Little skin could be seen under the blood that seemed to cover his whole body. It was a wonder he was still conscious.

Soon ants began to crawl onto Tom, but he ignored the pain as he dragged the man away from the ground where the ants had congregated in the bloody patch. He brought Simalala into the clearing and leaned him against a rock. The man wheezed as he attempted to speak. The ants who had traveled with him continued to gnaw away at him and attempted to bring down their second victim as Tom swept them off his legs. His blood boiled in a rage that he could not control. He left Simalala and, like a freight train, went for Hansie, landing his fist squarely in the man's face and breaking his nose. The man staggered backward, and Tom followed it with a powerful punch to his stomach. He doubled over and fell on his side and then rolled onto his back, protecting his bleeding face. Leering above him, Tom kicked him hard in the ribs as the man screamed in pain. Hansie's face was now a mass of blood, and he writhed on the ground clutching his side. Mooi Boetie said nothing and did nothing. He had no sympathy for the man. Simalala's cry once again pierced the atmosphere.

Tom returned to his friend to watch his chest rise and fall in quick shudders as he gasped for breath. There was nothing he could do. Time stood still for a moment as he stared at the broken and torn body of a warrior, a strong, brave, and capable man, a leader of his people. He was reminded that some tribes condemned adulterous couples to a fate such as this, and he had once seen a cow consumed by these Serewe ants down to the carcass. It was a torturous way to die for any living creature, least of all this man, his friend. Tom knew there was no way to kill them but to burn them, but how could such a thought pervade his mind as his friend still had breath in his body.

His eyes welled as he stared down at this shell of the man who had been by his side in some of his darkest hours. He thought of family, his children, and his village. Simalala lifted his arm towards Tom, and he clutched it. The bridge that formed between their arms allowed the ants to travel from Simalala to Tom, but he endured it, if not to share in his suffering for just a moment. Mooi Boetie approached with the revolver in hand, and Simalala looked at it longingly.

The revolver was passed from Mooi Boetie to Tom and into Simalala's hand, who curled his finger around the trigger. "I will never forget you, my friend. You are a great warrior. I will avenge your father, and your people will know of your bravery." Tom promised, and he moved the barrel against Simalala's temple and quickly moved away from the man before he changed his mind.

As he walked away into the clearing, the gunshot reverberated, and Tom dropped to the ground in a guttural scream. Even as the bites from the ants that still crawled on him grew more intense, Tom remained there like a statue, almost numb to the tragedy of it all.

"Sutton!" came a desperate call from behind him. Mooi Boetie was on the ground, and Hansie had Tom's revolver in his hand. Tom stood to take in the scene, and then out of nowhere, Hansie let out a blood-curdling scream. Hundreds of ants had gravitated from Simalala's dead body to his bloodied one. He dropped the gun and desperately tried to pull off his clothing, but it was too late. The ants had already made it up his torso and were beginning to eat away at his face. He jumped around madly, but that only made them more pervasive. Mooi Boetie and Tom looked on as the large man came crashing to his knees, as the colony invaded his body. Neither could nor would do anything to help him.

Mooi Boetie broke the silence. "Mr. Byrne is badly hurt he is up there at that tree, way back there. Bradley took the boy and your Heidi."

Tom nodded, his brow furrowed in worry.

"You're going to have to douse that with petrol and set it on fire. That's all you can do." Mooi shook his head knowingly, but he was in no rush to speed up Hansie's death.

Weasel saw Tom approach and called out to him through gasps of breath.

"Took you long enough, Boyo?"

"I'm sorry. How bad is it, Weasel?"

"Ah, not that bad…." Weasel lied as he coughed and winced at the pain in his side.

Tom pulled away Heidi's makeshift bandage. He could see the bullet hole.

"I need to get you to a doctor Weasel."

"I'm sorry about Simalala Tom. He was a good man…a good friend. It was a horrible way to die." said Weasel changing the subject. He, too had heard the African wailing and had witnessed Hansie's cruelty from his vantage point before he had passed out.

"No, he didn't deserve to die this way, especially at the hands of these cowards," said Tom wiping a tear from his face.

Hansie's screams permeated the very air around them now, but Tom felt nothing.

"He almost killed Mooi Boetie too. If anyone deserves to die like that, he does." said Weasel wearily. "Bradley has the kids, Tom. He's going to kill them…he's heading to the Falls. You have to hurry."

"Come on then," said Tom urgently. He practically lifted Weasel up and onto his shoulder.

"You don't have time for me. I have wasted my youth trying to mature you. You know this bullet is deep in my gut must have a fist-size hole now. You can't change this."

"I'm not leaving you, god-damnit!"

"You lost Sean once before because of me, I won't let you lose him again. He's headed to the Falls, go…go now."

"Not without you, Weasel."

"Then get me into that car. I may have one last adventure left in me." He said weakly, mustering a smile.

Tom carried Weasel to the car like a newborn baby and placed him in the passenger seat. Mooi Boetie had been slowly extricating petrol from the tank.

"You are sure you're ok? The Police can't be more than twenty minutes behind me. Explain to them what happened. I will take responsibility for what happened to Hansie. My horses should be up there on the road, too, somewhere." Mooi Boetie nodded.

"Take care of Timothy." he smiled weakly as the truck peeled out of the clearing.

He moved back to where Hansie lay. He was barely alive. The ants had almost completely ravaged his face, and the army had tripled in size. Mooi took the petroleum and poured it liberally over both men's bodies, one who no longer felt any pain and the other that dwelled within it. He lit a match and dropped it.

"Thomas Sutton killed no one."

CHAPTER 18

THE LOVERS' LEAP

Heidi and John bumped around mercilessly in the back as Bradley's truck moved along at a fair clip. Bradley was careful to keep his distance from Tom, who he presumed was about thirty minutes ahead of him. He was happy that nightfall would not be in Tom's or the police's favor. These roads were unpredictable in the daylight and almost hazardous at night, especially in their vehicles. But the cloak of the night had proved to be somewhat advantageous for the prisoners too. With Bradley's vision curtailed, John had managed to untie himself, but Heidi's hands were still too tightly bound, and the car too bumpy to make further progress without him noticing.

Bradley wasn't panicked yet, but as he gripped the steering wheel, slightly drunk on whisky, his mind began conjuring a frightful conclusion. He couldn't deny that the presence of the police hadn't shaken him. What if they had caught Hansie? Would he have ratted him out? Or worse, what if Tom had some evidence of his indiscretions and one of the witnesses had survived? The gold, his life's obsession, was the least of his problems now. This was about his freedom and, ultimately, his life. He tried to shake these troubling thoughts from his mind, but his calculating side was always skewed towards self- preservation. He had enough cash on him to make a run for it, he decided. He could cross the bridge at the Falls tonight and catch the train to the Cape the next morning and be on board a ship to England before anyone realized.

* * * *

The rough and uneven roadway, coupled with spotty vision, made the journey almost unbearable for Weasel. Each bump and jerk sent searing pain into his side that made his chest hurt for want of breath. Each time Tom tried to slow down the Buick in response, Weasel protested.

"We don't have time. Just go!" he urged through gasps of breath.

"Hang on, Weasel. We will soon be on the service road, and it shall get better."

They had managed to cross the dry sand and the Nanzela River. But each time Tom looked at his friend, he seemed paler and weaker.

"I am really sorry, Tom, I kept you away from Sean. If I had known, I would never have..." he trailed off

"Of course, you wouldn't have. You owe me no apologies, Tim. You saved my life." Tom said earnestly as he patted Weasel's hand. "Now stop talking and keep pressure on that wound."

Weasel smiled wearily.

"I'm taking the back road to the Falls. The one that you and Mooi Boetie told me about. Can you show me?"

"You're putting a lot of trust in this car, Tom."

"I know, but it's our only chance of heading him off if he's going straight to the Falls." Tom gripped the steering wheel tightly and placed the car in top gear as they bumped onto the service road.

"Tom, there is something I need you to promise me."

"Tim, don't talk," begged Tom, tears coming to the corners of his eyes.

"Ah, you haven't called me that in fifteen years. This must be serious," Weasel said with a smile.

"Tom. Go to Izzy. He'll know what to do. You are my next of kin...the money is yours...but don't be a greedy bastard and share some of it with the kids. Make sure Sean and Heidi are happy." He coughed as he eked out the last few words.

Tears blurred Tom's vision as he tried to navigate the road in front of him.

"Don't talk like that, you ejeet. You'll be well enough to have your own money." scolded Tom sucking back his tears.

"My life has always been an adventure with you, my friend. I can't say it hasn't been exciting." he coughed, trying to laugh.

Here he was, sitting next to him, making light of his own death, that scrawny little boy in knickerbockers who Tom had never been fast enough to catch. He remembered how broken Weasel had been when his brother Shamus had been killed, and he thought he might never overcome that grief. He felt that way now.

Tom had become Weasel's project. It was his trauma that had given Weasel the strength to move forward and ultimately save them both in the process. Tom had never had siblings, but this man beside him had been more than a brother to him, he had been his countryman, his partner, and his savior so many times in his life. Weasel had always needed a purpose, and he refused to let him die this way, so Tom pulled back his tears and insisted the man ready himself for battle.

The Buick arrived at the Falls ahead of Bradley, as they had both hoped. Weasel hadn't spoken for the last few miles, and his breathing was shallower.

The Buick had come to rest at the very spot Heidi and John had visited months ago. The voluminous falls gushed in front of them, and the sky was bright with stars. The powerful falls cared not for the guilt or innocence of its victims. It had been here long before humans and their strife. It communed only with the sky in all its beauty.

Tom reversed the car behind the tree and shut off the lights, checking to make sure they had left no visible tracks. They had a clear view from this vantage point. He pulled a cigarette from his pocket and lit it, placing it between Weasel's lips.

Weasel sighed. It was a blessing to dilute the taste of blood in his mouth with sweet tobacco.

"Weasel, when Bradley is away from the car, hit the lights. That will blind him, and then I can take him down. Element of surprise. Like old times." Tom said, half smiling.

Weasel closed his eyes to affirm his understanding before Tom leaned in and gently embraced his friend.

"You are my brother Weasel. My family…you always have been," said Tom, teary-eyed as he leaned in to embrace the man.

"Enough with the talk, Thomas. I'm not dead yet. Move me to the driver's seat." coughed Weasel as Tom helped him maneuver into the driver's seat. Tom didn't see the blood Weasel coughed up as a truck engine and headlights moved towards them. Tom crouched low to the ground behind the tree, out of sight. When the truck stopped, he could see Heidi and Sean crouched on the back of the flatbed. They seemed to be tied up, but they were still alive. What happened next took them both by surprise. As Bradley opened the door and jumped on the footboard, John stood up and smashed him hard in the head with the rock. As Bradley stumbled backward, John rushed to untie Heidi. The roar of the Falls gushed before them, tumbling thousands of feet into invisibility.

"I am here, Bradley. Come and get me," said Tom in the darkness from his hiding place behind the tree. As Bradley staggered to his feet, John screamed. "He has a gun."

Bradley shot in Tom's direction, but he had already crawled back behind the tree. During the scuffle, John had managed to free Heidi, and together, they had scrambled off the truck and crawled away in the opposite direction, keeping the vehicle between themselves and Bradley.

Bradley moved away from the truck, waving his gun wildly in Tom's direction. Blood now spilled from Weasel's mouth as he coughed, but he managed to hit the switch. Bright light assaulted Bradley, and his eyes darted from side to side in fits of fear. He looked so small against the backdrop of the mighty Falls and the wide black African sky behind him.

As Bradley placed his hand over his eyes to shield them from the light, Weasel put the car into gear and placed his foot onto the accelerator. He forced the pedal down until it touched the floor of the car and steered straight at Bradley. Bradley saw nothing but the blinding light until the heavy metal bonnet made contact. His abominable head pierced the windshield, and Weasel slumped in his seat, letting go of the steering wheel.

Tom, who had managed to scramble to his feet, screamed at the moving vehicle. John and Heidi looked on in horror as the vehicle maintained its momentum with Bradley stuck in the windshield. Tom ran after the car almost all the way to the edge just in time to see Weasel close his eyes for the last time, a satisfied smile etched on his face, as the Buick nose-dived into the belly of the mighty Mosi-oa-Tunya disappearing into the boiling pot below.

The three of them gathered at the edge and stared. The waters roared below, and the fog and spray engulfed them. It was a sight of terror, wonder, and unfathomable loss. John took off his jacket and draped it around Heidi's shoulders. Bitter tears now drenched all their cheeks. Tom came to stand between them, placing his left arm around John and his right around Heidi, and he pulled them close to him.

"He was my brother. He was our family." Tom choked.

"He will always be with us… in our hearts Uncle Tom…forever," said Heidi as she buried her wet face in Tom's shoulder.

"Mammy will watch over him," said John as he stared out at the bright stars that twinkled majestically over the Falls.

"She always did, my boy…she always did."

"Can you ever forgive me, father? John whispered after a few moments.

"You have already been forgiven, Sean. No one can change the past, son. We can only look to the future now. I take it you love Heidi.

"I do, sir."

"And you love him, Heidi?"

"Very much," said Heidi smiling at John.

"Well, if it's my blessing you're after, you have it."

Father and son embraced. The spray from the falls descended like the mist of baptism upon them, and the sins of their collective past seemed to wash away. Heidi stood apart and watched this reconciliation between the two men she cared for most in her life. She said a silent prayer of thanks to God and to her father for watching over them. It was nothing short of a miracle that the three of them had survived this ordeal.

It wasn't long before their peace was broken by the sound of sirens approaching. Three police vehicles arrived on the scene polluting the beautiful night sky with flashing lights and garish sounds. The first car door opened, and Len emerged, pistol in hand, followed by several deputies from the other cars. When he assessed the scene before him, he had the men lower their weapons. The passenger door of the chief's vehicle opened, and the Major got out. When John saw him, he ran to him like a child and threw his arms around him. Heidi followed, and John introduced her.

Tom felt a hand on his shoulder.

"He's gone, Len. Right into the Falls." Tom said numbly. "By the looks of things, he took Bradley with him." Tom nodded slightly.

"Let's get going now, Thomas."

"The boy is innocent, Len."

"I know."

"I want you to come with me to the police station?"

"For killing Hansie?"

"Of course not. Mooi Boetie told me everything. What you did was barely self-defense. Besides, I saw what was left of the bodies after the ants. I can't tell you how happy I am to see the three of you alive."

"No doubt you heard about the gold. I want to make sure it is returned to Simalala's village." Tom mumbled almost incoherently.

"Of course," said Len. "Now, come with me to the station. Maria is waiting for you."

When they arrived at the station, Maria was waiting there with Mooi Boetie. She leaped into Tom's arms as soon as he was out of the car and showered Heidi and John with kisses and warm embraces.

"Where is Timothy?" she asked, looking anxiously from one face to the next.

"He didn't make it, Maria," said Tom with wet eyes.

"He saved our lives," added John

"Oh, Thomas. I am so sorry."

"And Simalala too," he said softly, and Maria cried, burying her face in his chest.

"Are you sure you won't spend the night here in town, Tom," Len argued when Tom decided they would head back to Demberra that night.

"Len, I just want to go home."

"But your house is a mess, Sutton. Be reasonable."

"It's alright, Len," whispered Maria.

"I will stay here for a couple of days if that's alright, Uncle Tom. The Major has kindly reserved a couple of rooms at the hotel. John and I will come home on the weekend when the Major returns to Salisbury."

"We want to make some wedding plans before he heads back," John added.

"Of course," said Tom as he shook the Major's hand. The men exchanged a look of mutual admiration before they parted ways.

Maria and Tom waved as Heidi and John walked hand in hand alongside the Major towards the hotel. Heidi turned and blew them a kiss.

"They were meant to be." smiled Maria

"I believe you are right, my love," he said and kissed her hand gently.

One of Len's African constables was tasked with driving the couple home. Despite the chaos and tragedy of the last two days, the night seemed strangely peaceful, and Tom's heart, despite all the pain, was full of love and gratitude.

When they got out of the car at Kabi Siding, and the constable turned around and headed back to Livingstone, Tom and Maria stood and stared at the skeletal house that had once been their glorious home.

"Thomas, I have been waiting a long to tell you something," Maria confessed.

"Please Maria, before you say anything…there is something I need to tell you… something I should have said a long time ago. I love you, and I need you, Maria. I need you in my life now and always. Please say you will be my wife."

Maria's eyes filled with tears. "You are going to be a father again. And, of course, I will marry you, Thomas."

Tom was overwhelmed. He cupped his hands around her face and kissed her. Then he took his hand and placed it protectively on her stomach.

"A baby." He said, his eyes glistening with joy.

"Our baby," she said as she placed her hands over his.

As they walked up the hill to the Dutchman's house. Tom's mind was already racing. He thought of Mooi Boetie, who would need employment now that Weasel was gone. With his help and Weasel's gift, he could begin again and rebuild Demberra. He could already envision robust bougainvillea climbing the pagoda again and the laughter of friends and family gathered on the verandah as he looked out over thriving crops and healthy herds. He would build a farm that his little son or daughter would thrive on and a homestead where Heidi and John could start a family of their own. He smiled at Maria and clutched her hand tightly. He looked up at the stars and searched for Grace. He whispered, "Thank you for giving me back my son, and thank you for giving me the strength to love again. You're free, Grace. Until we meet again."

THE END